JUST IN TIME!

Ruthie felt the bite of rope against her bare skin.

"Reckon we better tie your ankles," Sheriff Rudd muttered, and bent down.

Two men boosted a third man high enough to place a noose about Ruthie's neck and draw it tight.

"All right," Rudd said, "kick it out from under her."

At that moment, he saw a horseman come pounding out of the trees, gripping a rifle.

"Lassiter!" Rudd cried, standing stiffly.

"I came on ahead," he said thinly, sliding to the ground. "Looks like I'm in time…."

LOREN ZANE GREY

LASSITER

LEISURE BOOKS   NEW YORK CITY

LEISURE BOOKS ®

December 2004

Published by

Dorchester Publishing Co., Inc.
200 Madison Avenue
New York, NY 10016

Originally published by Pocket Books, 1985.

ISBN 0-8439-5418-3

Printed in the United States of America.

Visit us on the web at www.dorchesterpub.com.

LASSITER

1

LASSITER WAS SCOUTING AHEAD of the DL herd that was lumbering up through a long valley about a mile back when he suddenly came upon a wrecked wagon. It lay at the foot of a long and very steep grade. Not much of a road, really—little more than a pair of wheel tracks through this wilderness of northern Arizona.

Urging his black horse through a stand of stunted oaks, he reined in and studied the wreck. Both front wheels of the wagon had been smashed and the tongue torn off in the crash. The accident had happened so recently that a haze of dust still hovered about the wreckage, not yet blown away by the afternoon breeze.

He saw the team, frothy and bearing fresh whip marks, hung up a short distance away by the wagon tongue. It was turned sideways against some saplings, trapping the animals.

Lassiter swung his tall, lithe figure out of the saddle and started for them. And then as he cleared the wagon he saw the crumpled figure of a man on the far side. Lassiter's dark eyes studied the man's handsome face, which had a touch of the brute about it. The man was lying on his back, arms outflung, head twisted at an odd angle, indicating a broken neck. There was blood at his lips. Even so, Lassiter stopped and felt for a pulse. There was none. He straightened up, looking the stranger over. A well-dressed man probably in his early thirties, wearing a yellow suit that was torn and coated with dust. The eyes were wide open in savage surprise.

Lassiter saw where the wagon had plowed through chaparral. A pungent odor of greasewood still hung in the air. Lassiter's skin was dark, not from his heritage but from sun and weather. An inch under six feet, he was solidly built at a hundred and seventy-five pounds. Black hair curled from under the brim of a flat-crowned sombrero set squarely on his head. His dark blue eyes could be filled with humor or coldness, depending on the occasion. He had a high-beaked nose above a mouth too wide to brand him as handsome. He was broad through the shoulders, tapering to a narrow, gun-belted waist.

A sound came from somewhere behind the wagon— possibly a sob but he couldn't be sure. And in this lonely stretch of country surrounded by towering mountains, he was taking no chances.

A .44 snapped into his hand. "Come out of there," he ordered harshly so there would be no mistake.

There was a movement in the brush as a girl in a torn blue dress emerged. A straw bonnet fastened to thick dark hair had been crushed against her skull. One eye was faintly purplish and swollen. But it looked more like an old injury and not one suffered in the wreck. As she drew nearer he saw that the sleeves of her dress had been pushed up, probably because of the heat, exposing rounded forearms. On each of them were several fresh lash marks. She saw him looking and gingerly pushed down the sleeves to cover them.

"He did that to you?" Lassiter asked, jerking his head at the dead man.

"He did." She stood, looking forlorn, eyes on the ground.

"Jealousy, I suppose," Lassiter said. "Was that the reason?"

That brought her head swinging up. "God knows, anything but that," she said brokenly.

"Then why did he beat you?"

"He . . . he accused me of holding back some of the money I earned. . . ." Then she caught herself and said quickly, "He . . . he was a gambler. I helped him." She looked away, wiping her eyes.

Somehow it lacked the ring of truth. She looked to be in her early twenties with dark gray eyes. Finally meeting Lassiter's skeptical gaze caused her shoulders to slump.

"Oh, what's the use," she said with a weary gesture. "You can guess our business. I was his . . . his girl." That brought on a spate of tears that streamed across her rather attractive face and dampened the front of the blue dress.

Lassiter was going through the dead man's pockets as he asked how the wreck had happened. Finally, she got herself under control enough to explain about her companion who had been in a rage and driven too fast down the grade. She gestured at the high hill where the road curved at her back.

"I begged Pete to slow down and that's when he started using a quirt on me. . . ." She shuddered at the memory. "At the foot of the hill we hit a rut. "I . . . I was thrown out. But the wagon flipped over on him. Then I heard you coming and hid. . . ."

In the dead man's pockets he found a few letters, some change and nine silver dollars. Getting up, he tried to hand them to her, but she waved away the letters.

"I . . . I don't want them." But she did let him drop the change and the silver dollars into her cupped hands.

"How'd you happen to be on this God-forsaken stretch of road?" It certainly wasn't well traveled; weeds had overgrown the ruts.

"Pete thought he was taking a shortcut," she explained, knuckling her eyes. "We got lost. That's when he flew into a rage."

"When'd he give you the black eye?"

"A week ago." She stared down at the dead man. "I should be sorry he's dead, but . . ." She drew a deep breath and let her words drift away. "Can you take me with you?"

"To where?"

"Just anywhere." Her reddened eyes met his. She tried for a tremulous smile that didn't fit her quivering, heavily rouged mouth.

Lassiter thought it over. There was no telling when anybody would come along this lonely stretch of country.

"You'll have to come with us," Lassiter told her, then explained that he was half owner of a herd of cattle on the move from New Mexico to this far corner of Arizona.

By then the clack of cattle hooves could be heard, the grunt and bellow of the leaders, the shouts of riders urging them up the steep grade of the valley. Pinions dotted the rim of red rock. A banner of dust floated down the long valley to mark the passage of the thousand head of beef.

"Please don't tell the men about me," she implored. "With Pete dead . . . I want to make a fresh start."

His generous mouth smiled. "Sure I'll keep quiet. You do likewise. I don't want the men fighting over you. What's your name, by the way?"

"Ruthie."

"All right, Ruthie, I'll see that you get to Wayfield. That's the nearest settlement."

By then, Lassiter's partner, Owney Devlin, was charging upgrade through the chaparral on a horse large enough to support his weight. "What we got here?" he demanded, as he saw Ruthie, the dead man and the wrecked wagon.

"She was traveling with her husband when the team ran away," Lassiter said blandly.

Eddie Pyne came riding up on a sweated buckskin in time to hear Lassiter's explanation of what had happened. Not far out of his teens, Pyne packed a load of youthful arrogance on lean shoulders. A patch of pale hair was sweat-plastered to his forehead. Wild blue eyes in a long and usually sullen face brightened when he saw Ruthie standing beside the wagon.

Then he glanced at the dead man lying in the road. "You claim he's her husband, Lassiter?" Pyne said with a laugh. "Don't see no weddin' ring on her finger."

"She said she had to sell it to buy food," Lassiter said quickly and noted the grateful look Ruthie gave him.

The herd lumbered on past them, driven by the four-man crew. At last came the swaying wagon, gray-bearded Tom Hefter handling the reins. The old man drew up and looked quizzically at Ruthie. Tears had streaked through powder on her cheeks.

"She'll sleep in the wagon," Lassiter said after explaining that she was going with them. Everybody stays clear of her." His gaze snapped to Devlin's nephew. "Understood, Eddie?"

Eddie Pyne only mumbled something, but his uncle said, "I agree to that."

Lassiter got a shovel from the wagon and started to dig a grave. He was glad the matter had been settled so easily. It had been a long, hard pull out of New Mexico, the crew's only pleasure being the one drink Devlin allowed them before supper each evening. They had endured one stampede which set them back several days and almost suffered a second one. And all this time the crew had been womanless. Having Ruthie around for the last portion of the trip couldn't help but add to the tension.

That evening Ruthie, wearing a bandanna over her glossy hair to keep off the dust, helped Tom Hefter with the cooking. The old man was glad to have such a "purty" assistant.

Lassiter and Devlin and the latter's nephew, Eddie Pyne, were sprawled on the ground, eating. When they finished they'd relieve the others who would come in for supper. Ruthie was moving about with the coffee pot for refills. When Eddie Pyne reached out to touch her ankle, he was instantly aware of Lassiter's dark gaze. Pyne flushed and removed his hand. Ruthie continued her rounds, wearing a faint smile.

Pyne said angrily, "Don't do no harm to touch a gal, does it?"

"In this case it does," Lassiter said.

"Uncle Owney, you figure to let him run things?" Pyne demanded of his uncle.

"He's my partner," Devlin reminded his nephew. "We both run things."

Before riding out, Lassiter spoke quietly to Hefter. "Take care of her, Tom," nodding in Ruthie's direction. Not that she probably needed taking care of now that she had recovered from her shock. She seemed self-sufficient, a quality which Lassiter admired. In addition to that, she was cheerful and insisted on doing her share of the work.

After he and Devlin had relieved the four hands, Lassiter looked over the shadowed herd bathed in starlight and the faint glow of a sickle moon. This bunch of cattle represented his latest gamble; a chance at long last to lead a reasonably normal life and put down roots. Women had been telling him that for so long that he had finally decided to give it a try.

The opportunity came when his old friend, Owney Devlin, expressed an urge to quit New Mexico and move onto a ranch he'd bought earlier in the year in northern Arizona. But Devlin in his negotiations soon got in over his head. He urged Lassiter to come in with him.

"A chance for the two of us to start new lives in new

territory," was how Devlin eagerly explained it. What it came down to was the fact that Devlin had cattle and a ranch of sorts but lacked the cash to relocate. He happened to catch Lassiter with a full money sack. Lassiter was generous.

He was technically a drifter because he never seemed able to stay in one place long enough to "take a deep breath," as Devlin would say. Women were intrigued by him. Men found him likable, a good companion and staunch friend. Those who listened to his enemies were inclined to believe the worst. There were times when he was incredibly lucky at cards. Then would come the long, dry spells. From the first, he was determined to make the most of his partnership with Owney Devlin.

But a faint shadow was cast on the partnership when Devlin had spoken belatedly of his arrangement with one Eloise Hartney, hemming and hawing as he explained how he had seen her picture in a catalogue and over the weeks had corresponded.

"A picture bride," Lassiter said with a grim smile.

"You make it sound like somethin' bad."

"Don't mean to, Owney. It's a fact of life out here. There're more men than women."

When he and Devlin reached the herd, Eddie Pyne was cussing out a couple of longhorns that had strayed into the brush. Devlin, chuckling, rode up to his nephew. "We'll soon be havin' a lady around the house, so you better watch your cussin'."

"Oh, hell, Uncle Owney, I'd never cuss around sweet Eloise. You reckon she'll be as purty as her picture?"

"Prettier," Devlin said, then grew silent for a few moments. "Hope she makes the long trip out here all right."

"Maybe she run off with the money you sent her, Uncle Owney," Eddie Pyne chided, which angered Devlin.

"Goddamn it, start circlin' that herd an' keep your mouth shut about Eloise."

"Now who's cussin?" With a hoot of laughter, Eddie rode off into the darkness.

"Once we're settled, I'll have time to cool him down a mite," Devlin said. He removed his hat and forked fingers through a mop of ginger-colored hair. "My sister was his ma an' all I got to remember her by is Eddie." Devlin choked up as usual whenever he spoke about his dead sister.

The first Lassiter had heard about Eddie was two months ago when he and Devlin had become partners. Eddie Pyne had been living with an old maid aunt in Missouri.

"Me wantin' to get outa New Mexico is for Eddie's sake," Devlin had explained. "An' for my sake. Here there's memories of his ma an' how she died. Soon as we're settled, I'll send for him."

Actually, Lassiter had looked forward to passing along to a young boy information gleaned from a lifetime on the range. Lassiter was under the impression that Eddie was much younger. Even Devlin was surprised at his nephew's size when he showed up unexpectedly at the place in New Mexico just as Devlin and Lassiter were about to pull out. Eddie, scared out of his wits, blurted that his aunt was dead and that shortly after her funeral he had shot it out with a man on a Missouri street, killing him. A man who was a member of a particularly vindictive family.

Only after the kid decided there was no threat from Missouri did his cockiness emerge. Lassiter kept telling himself that when the time came, Devlin would settle his nephew down. But even so, Lassiter felt a vague sense of disaster looming ahead.

The following morning Eddie Pyne shouted, "Company comin'!"

Lassiter, taking his turn riding drag, jerked down the bandanna that covered the lower half of his face because of the dust. Not knowing what to expect in such a remote stretch of country, he eased his rifle in the boot and spurred past the herd. They were moving up a long grade bordered by gnarled and twisted junipers. Cliff walls of pale gray limestone were splashed by sunlight.

Five riders were sitting in their saddles some distance ahead. Devlin was leaning from his horse to offer a calloused hand for a powerfully built man to shake. Lassiter's face hardened as he recognized the man.

"It's Joe Rudd," Devlin called to Lassiter. "One of our new neighbors."

Lassiter slowed his horse and approached at a walk. Rudd had detached himself from his four riders who had moved off under some ponderosas.

"First I heard about Joe Rudd being a neighbor," Lassiter said coolly, reining in. He didn't offer his hand.

Rudd smiled thinly. "I didn't tell Devlin when he was up pokin' around here this spring, lookin' for a ranch to buy, that you and me are old . . . friends. That right, Lassiter?"

2

LASSITER'S SILENCE MADE DEVLIN nervous. "So you know each other? By damn."

"Sort of," Lassiter drawled. He looked over at Rudd's four riders. The usual hard-eyed crew, especially the little dark-faced man who was squinting at him against the sun.

"Welcome to Arizona, Lassiter," Rudd said pleasantly, a big brown-haired man of thirty-five or so. A faded red vest was held together by a heavy gold watch chain. His shirt was white, his pants fawnskin. An ivory-butted .45 rode in a holster at his belt. Today Rudd was as genial as he had been four years before in a courtroom when denying a charge of rustling horses. How absurd that a man of his stature could be considered a common horse thief was the message he tried to impart to the jury. The horses in question, over four hundred head, owned by a friend of Lassiter's, were being driven to a Texas ranch when Rudd was apprehended.

"Been watching for you," Rudd said. "My foreman spotted your dust. And here I am." Rudd cleared his throat. "Just figure to set things straight, you fellas being newcomers to the Diablo range." Then he went on to explain that four small ranchers had joined him in forming a pool along with his Hayfork Ranch. "They elected me to run it."

"What's the reason for the pool?" Lassiter asked quietly.

"It's the only way we can fight off the Kerringtons."

"Recollect Charlie Tolliver mentioning 'em when I was dickerin' to buy his ranch," Devlin put in.

"Would like to have you in the pool," Rudd said. "How about it, boys?"

Devlin fingered his heavy chin and cast a sidelong glance at his partner. "What you think, Lassiter?"

"These Kerringtons a real threat?" Lassiter asked Rudd.

"Mike Kerrington is crippled up. But the spread is run by his niece, Allie. A stubborn female if I ever saw one. But plenty tough when it comes to Kerrington domination of the Diablo range."

The herd had pushed past them but the wagon had become stuck in a dry creekbed some fifty yards away. Old Tom Hefter was trying to dig it out with a shovel. Ruthie was holding in the team.

"I'll go give Tom a hand," Lassiter announced, glad for an excuse to get away.

"We'll all lend a hand," Joe Rudd said cheerfully once he had ascertained the trouble. He ordered his four men to throw their shoulders behind the wheels of the wagon. With Lassiter's and Devlin's help, all that manpower freed it instantly.

"Thanks, Rudd," Devlin said, wiping his face on a bandanna.

Rudd was amusedly studying Ruthie, who had slid over in the seat to hand the reins to Hefter. "I see you're traveling with your own camp woman," Rudd remarked. "Good idea to keep the crew happy. . . ."

"She's a widow lady," Lassiter interrupted coolly. "Her husband was killed a few miles back, and we're seeing she gets to Wayfield."

"My mistake then," Rudd said. "With all that paint an' powder I naturally figured . . ."

Lassiter made a mental note to tell Ruthie to keep her face washed as long as she was with them.

"Well, remember one thing," Rudd said seriously. "We're all in this together against the Kerringtons. That right, Sid?"

He called to the small, wiry dark man with the cold eyes. It was his foreman, Sid Salone.

"You're right, boss," Salone replied and turned his back and mounted up.

When Rudd and his men had ridden off, Devlin said, "You two did everything but growl at each other."

"Wish I'd known Rudd was to be our neighbor. . . ."

"You mean you wouldn't have gone in with me if you'd have knowed that?"

Lassiter didn't reply.

"Tell me about you an' Rudd," Devlin urged. Here the country was rolling uplands coming up against a ridge of purple mountains. Gone were the canyons with red rock walls. They were on the Diablo range at last.

"I appeared as a witness against Rudd," Lassiter explained. "Four years ago." A jury, largely intimidated, had turned Rudd loose, Lassiter went on to say.

"Well, he was found innocent then." Devlin seemed relieved and rubbed the side of his face with a beefy hand. He was six feet three and weighed two hundred and twenty pounds.

"But I took the stand against him on the rustling charge. He's got a long memory."

"He's likely forgot all about that business of four years back," Devlin went on with forced joviality. "Hell, he never once brung it up."

"He will." Knowing that the rundown ranch here in northern Arizona that Devlin had bought in early spring shared Diablo range with Rudd did nothing to cheer Lassiter.

Later that day Rudd and his foreman were in the Four Aces, the larger, more ornate of the two saloons in Wayfield. The smaller one at the opposite end of Commerce Street was known as Matt's.

On this late afternoon there were few customers. Rudd's three cowhands were further down the long bar, drinking by themselves. Ed Cavendish, the owner, a dumpy man with outsized sideburns, was at the far end reading a newspaper.

Rudd and Salone had been discussing Lassiter in low voices. "The only answer is to get rid of him," Rudd said and bit down on a cigar.

"I'll handle him," Salone muttered, taking a hitch at his gunbelt. He had a little man's perpetual urge to prove himself. But Rudd got a grip on the man's wiry arm.

"Maybe you can handle him, maybe not. But I don't

want Hayfork involved. To play it safe, I think we'll get two men to bring him down."

"Who you got in mind?" the little foreman wanted to know.

"Bishop and Stillway, I'm thinkin' of."

"Them," Salone said through his teeth. "Kerrington men."

"But they've done good work for me a time or two," Rudd reminded Salone. "Been well paid, I might add."

Salone shrugged and kept his mouth shut. He had no use for the pair who had been on the Kerrington payroll for over a year. Even though Salone was no stranger to treachery and violence, he detested men who'd sell out their employer, as was the case with Bishop and Stillway when it came to the Kerringtons.

A few minutes earlier Rudd had seen Bishop and Stillway enter the Wayfield Mercantile down the block. Possibly they were still there, he told Salone.

"Go over and tell them to meet me out back of the livery barn in fifteen minutes," Rudd instructed.

Salone had been gone from the Four Aces only a few minutes when the southbound stage rolled into town with the usual cloud of dust and cacophony of barking dogs. Only one passenger alighted at the Wayfield House across the street. A rather demure-looking blonde wearing a soiled dust cloak. She was standing at the boot as the driver lifted out a small trunk which he placed on the walk. Then, with a wave of his hand, he drove away.

"Wonder who the blonde is?" Rudd said to Ed Cavendish, who had left his newspaper to come up to the bar.

"Might be she's the one Owney Devlin is expectin'," the saloonman said. "He left the herd that him an' his partner are pushin' toward the old Tolliver place an' come into town a few days back."

"Is it Devlin's wife?"

"Soon to be, accordin' to Devlin. A picture bride."

"Be damned," Rudd said and watched her follow the trunk that was being carried to the hotel. Through the front window he studied the sway of hips as the young lady hurried inside.

On his way to the livery barn, Rudd strolled past the hotel, glancing in at the compact lobby with its leather furniture. But he failed to see her.

Out behind the livery stable, Salone was waiting with two hard-eyed young men. They stood in a deep pool of shadow under cottonwoods.

Rudd shook hands with them. Hi Bishop, the younger, was completely bald despite being only in his early twenties. "Sid says you wanta see us," Bishop began, his small eyes already gleaming at the prospect of money Rudd would pay for a job.

"His name is Lassiter." Even mentioning the name put a thread of anger in Rudd's voice. "I want him dead."

Stillway rubbed at a deep scar on his right cheek. "How quick you want him dead?"

"The sooner the better," Rudd snapped. He described Lassiter, saying that he was partners with Owney Devlin and that they were pushing a herd onto the old Tolliver ranch.

"Good as done, Mr. Rudd," Hi Bishop said. "We'll watch our chance an' bring him down."

"Box him in is the best way. He's tough an' cagey."

"How much we get for takin' care of this Lassiter fella?" Bishop wanted to know. He had a cherubic face that belied his chief occupation—murder.

Rudd thought it over for a moment and decided to be generous. It was a job that had to be done because he could never stomach that arrogant Lassiter as a neighbor. Not after the annoying business of the rustled horses four years ago. And he could tell from Lassiter's manner today that he would never join the pool. Devlin, however, was another matter, easy to manipulate without Lassiter.

"A hundred dollars each for the job," Rudd said.

The mention of two hundred dollars caused an exchange of tight smiles between Bishop and the scarred Tex Stillway. Birds chirped in the cottonwoods and from the distance came ringing sounds of a hammer on metal from the blacksmith's shop.

After the business of Lassiter was settled and Bishop and Stillway had departed, Rudd told Salone to ride home. "I'm going to stay over in town tonight."

He didn't mention to Salone that he wanted another, closer look at Owney Devlin's picture bride.

Several days before, at Lassiter's urging, Devlin had left the herd and ridden ahead to Wayfield to see if Eloise Hartney had arrived yet from St. Louis. When Devlin returned, he seemed morose. "If she'd been there I coulda faced right up to her. I was primed for it. But when I found out she ain't come in yet, I'm startin' to git cold feet."

Lassiter tried to josh him out of his depression but without success. That day Devlin had a run-in with his nephew and when it was over he shook his head and said for the tenth time, "Kid's older'n I figured on. Hell, I thought he was just a little tyke. Years kinda slip away, I reckon."

Before supper that sundown, Tom Hefter doled out the men's ration of whiskey. As a partner, Lassiter could have all he wanted, but one was enough. Devlin didn't drink, which was a departure from some years back when they had first met.

Tonight Devlin looked longingly at the whiskey being poured and went stomping off into the brush.

Lassiter got Tom Hefter aside. "Tonight Owney acted as if he'd give his right arm for a drink," Lassiter said softly. "What changed him from a drinking man?"

Hefter, who had worked for Devlin's father, tamped tobacco into a pipe, saying that the incident went back a few years. "Eddie's folks was over for a Sunday dinner I cooked up, them livin' poorly at the time. Well, Owney an' Eddie's pa, they done some drinkin' an' got into a fist fight. Eddie's pa was no damn good. Owney's sister, a purty little thing, tried to separate 'em. Her husband Sam figured to go home. With Owney passed out, Sam hitched up a half-broke team to a wagon. I tried to tell Sam not to drive that team but he wouldn't listen. About a mile down the road the team ran away an' the wagon turned over. Sam an' his missus was killed. Eddie was thrown out."

"Devlin blames himself in a way?" Lassiter guessed.

"If he hadn't been dead drunk, he'd never have let his sister ride off with Sam drivin' that half-broke team of horses." Hefter gave a long sigh. "Owney ain't never had a drink from that day to this. Hope he never does."

Several evenings later Devlin was telling Ruthie about Eloise, how he had sent her money to take the steam cars west and then south by stagecoach.

"I tell you, Ruthie," Devlin exclaimed when they were eating, "everybody'll know she's a lady. My own mother came from St. Louis. That's mostly what decided me on Eloise. That an' the way she looked in her picture in that catalogue."

Eddie Pyne came stomping up to hear the last, taking a plate from Ruthie. "Lassiter, what you think of my Uncle Owney sendin' all the way to St. Louis to get him a woman he's never laid eyes on?"

"His business," Lassiter said shortly.

Devlin tried to laugh. "Simmer down, Eddie."

"I figure you're too trustin', Uncle Owney."

"Eat your supper, Eddie," Devlin said, still trying to make light of it. But Eddie wouldn't let it go.

"Here we're startin' a ranch in strange country an' right off you got a rock tied around your neck with this Eloise."

Lassiter tensed, expecting an explosion from Devlin. But his partner only gave a strained chuckle.

At first, after landing unannounced on his uncle's doorstep, Eddie had seemed eager to please. But after a week or so on the trail from New Mexico, he began to change, which caused Devlin to say that likely his old maid sister back in Missouri had spoiled Eddie something fierce.

Lassiter would second that. He had a strong hunch that Eddie and Devlin's bride might not get along too well.

The next morning they had another visit from Joe Rudd. This time he was alone with his foreman, Sid

Salone. At sight of Lassiter, Rudd looked momentarily disappointed, then became affable. "Well, I see you're still here," Rudd said.

"Didn't you expect me to be?"

"You've got a rep for movin' along, Lassiter." Rudd smiled.

The way Lassiter coldly eyed Rudd made Devlin nervous. He changed the subject. "Hope Charlie Tolliver got around to fixin' up the house a little. It was in our agreement that he would."

"Tolliver got himself killed," Rudd said.

Devlin's face fell. "Charlie Tolliver . . . dead?"

"He was caught with two tied-down calves and a running iron in the fire," Rudd explained.

"I can't believe that Tolliver was a rustler. . . ."

"He figured to quit the country an' take a little extra money with him," Rudd said blandly. "He was stealing from one of the members of the pool."

"You mean the pool killed him," Lassiter said quietly.

"We look after our own," Rudd replied. "Thought any more about joining up?"

"No, we haven't," Lassiter said.

"Well, keep an eye on your back trail," Rudd said to Lassiter with a tight smile.

"What do you mean by that?" Lassiter demanded, but Rudd pretended he hadn't heard. He was riding away with Salone and soon the pair were lost in a stand of oaks.

"Charlie Tolliver dead," Devlin muttered with a shake of his head. "I just can't believe it. Wonder if he done any work on the house at all?"

"We'll soon know," Lassiter said. He was staring at

the faint haze of dust among the trees that marked the passage of Rudd and his foreman.

Devlin, noting the direction of his gaze, said, "Wish you an' Rudd would try to get along. Otherwise everything is liable to blow higher than the moon."

Lassiter didn't say anything. But he had a feeling that Devlin might just be right.

3

ELOISE HARTNEY SOAKED HER body in the zinc tub
that had been carried to her room in the Wayfield
House. She found her thoughts drifting to Owney
Devlin, as they had periodically all the way West.
What would he be like? All she had was his picture
showing a big grinning man holding a rifle and standing
alongside a horse. Mr. Baxter, of the hotel, a cadaver-
ous, ill-humored man, said that Devlin had been in
several days previously, asking about her. Eloise
didn't even know what day it was; she had lost all
track of time.

When the chambermaid brought more hot water,
Eloise smiled and vowed to give the woman two bits,
which she could ill afford. All she had in the world was
a gold eagle and two silver dollars.

After her bath, she sat on the hotel veranda and
dried her hair in the clear Arizona air. She breathed
deeply, not missing the coal smoke of St. Louis. It had
been sheer desperation that had prompted her to spend
three dollars to insert her photograph in the catalogue
of "Picture Brides."

She hadn't really expected a reply, but received three. Owney Devlin appealed to her the most, a successful cattleman about to establish a new ranch in Arizona.

A woman stopped by her chair and said, "I understand you're to marry my new neighbor, Owney Devlin."

Eloise shaded her eyes against the waning sun and looked up to see a tall young woman with auburn hair smiling down at her. "I'm Allie Kerrington." She had large, even teeth and a handsome face.

They shook hands. Allie Kerrington had a firm grip that surprised Eloise.

"I'm so used to being around men," Allie apologized, "I sometimes forget to be a lady. Would you take supper with me?"

"I . . . I'd like that." Eloise was taken in by the woman's forceful personality. A hat hung on the back of Allie's head from a chin strap. She wore a man's shirt and straight-legged Levis, boots with spurs that chimed as she dashed into the hotel to change her clothes.

An hour later in the hotel dining room, Eloise marveled at the difference in Allie, who now wore a dress of pale yellow. Her hair was done up, giving her a regal look. Large silver earrings reflected the lamplight.

"Why . . . you're beautiful," Eloise exclaimed.

Allie laughed. "Probably I should wear a dress more often. But I'd look silly herding cattle in one."

Soon they were talking about their lives and families. Allie had lost all of hers except for an uncle. In hushed tones Eloise spoke of her own loss, a family that had never recovered from the war.

"At least you have an uncle," Eloise said, spooning a thick soup.

"Don't forget you'll have a husband," Allie put in with a faintly bitter smile.

"Yes, I forgot about that," Eloise said nervously.

Midway through their meal, Joe Rudd stopped by their table. He maintained a room at the hotel on an annual basis, as did the Kerringtons. Although there was bitterness between them, Allie greeted him pleasantly and introduced Eloise.

"Charmed, Miss Hartney." Rudd bowed over her hand. He had changed into a tan suit, the ever-present watch chain of thick gold links draped across his flat stomach.

When Allie failed to ask him to join them, a shadow of irritation crept into his brown eyes. He soon moved to the far side of the room where two members of his pool were taking their supper. He joined them.

"I sensed that you're not fond of Mr. Rudd," Eloise remarked as she forked a sliver of beef into her pretty mouth.

"He once asked me to marry him. I rather imagine it stung his pride when I turned him down."

"I should think so, being rejected by an attractive girl."

"Thank you for the 'girl' part," Allie said with a small laugh. "But it was the prospect of adding our ranch to his that interested him more than me personally." She glanced across the room at Rudd's wide back in his tan coat. "He's become my enemy."

"In what way?"

"He's formed a pool to fight us."

Eloise looked bewildered. "Pool?"

Allie explained that it was an organization of ranchers. "They're dupes but I doubt if any of them have awakened to that fact as yet."

"I see."

"I'm hoping you can convince your new husband to be our friend, not our enemy."

"I'll do my best, although I don't know him . . ." Eloise broke off in confusion and explained in detail her arrangement with Devlin. "I hope to be a dutiful wife. But now that the moment is approaching I'm afraid I'm losing my nerve."

"Nonsense, you'll do fine." Allie's eyes were suddenly distant, piercing the walls of the grubby little frontier dining room as she thought about her own betrothal. Tod, whom she had met in the East, had come out to learn the cattle business before they married. But he was so inept. He was trampled to death in a stampede.

She told the story to Eloise who sat with tears glistening in her wide blue eyes.

"But enough of that." Allie gave the table top such a hard slap that the men at the far end of the dining room turned in their chairs.

The two women talked for another few minutes, then Eloise excused herself, pleading weariness from the long journey. After Eloise had gone to her room, Allie sat drinking coffee until she heard the familiar thump of her Uncle Mike's two canes. It meant he had finished drinking with his cronies at the Four Aces and would want to go home.

By the light of an early moon she drove the buckboard back to K-27. Most of the way her uncle complained about his aches and the fact that she hadn't married, which would bring a younger man into the family.

"Next time that Joe Rudd asks you, marry him, you hear me, Allie? I swear you're stubborn as your ma was. . . ."

"Rudd won't ask me again, Uncle Mike."

"Then I'll have a talk with him."

"You stay out of it."

"Rudd should be persistent. In my day, if a young man was turned down he kept on and on and gradually wore the young lady down. And don't you tell me to stay out of what is my business!"

"Joe Rudd is no friend of ours, as you well know."

"Come to think of it, I guess he isn't," her uncle admitted after a long silence. Then he bristled, the cracked old voice rising, "I'll take forty men and wipe that Joe Rudd off the face of Arizona Territory!"

"Uncle Mike, K-27 doesn't have the power it used to have. We no longer have forty men on the payroll, only eight." And we're lucky to have that many, she silently amended.

All the way home the clip-clop sounds of the horses' hooves of her escorts, Hi Bishop and Tex Stillway, were behind the wagon. Occasionally, Allie could hear their coarse laughter. It reminded her to have a talk with them.

They were on hand to help her uncle down from the wagon in front of the house. He hobbled on inside the house, the weight of his frail body supported by his twin canes.

She stayed by the wagon until her uncle was in the house, the heavy front door closed. Bishop and Stillway waited to take the wagon down to the barn.

She thoroughly disliked both of them but realized that in her circumstances riders were hard to come by; they sometimes had to wait for their pay.

"When you're in town after this, I want you to do your drinking at Matt's. Stay out of the Four Aces."

"Why's that?" Hi Bishop whined, watching her lovely eyes, which he could see in the lamplight spilling from the front window of the ranch house.

"Because Joe Rudd and his crowd drink in the Four Aces." She paused, letting her eyes pass from one face to the other. "Rudd seems to know a lot about what goes on out here. Pass the word to the other men, if you will," she finished crisply and went into the house.

In her room she started to undress, feeling tired, as usual. The evening had started well. Meeting Eloise had been a respite from what she had to face on a daily basis managing the ranch, blocking moves by Rudd and his pool, coping with cattle losses. They were explained away when Joe Rudd found Charlie Tolliver with two of her calves tied up at a branding fire. One of her K-27 brands was partially worked into an X-88 by a running iron heating in the fire.

Tolliver was shot in the back. After Tolliver's death last month, there were no more losses until a week ago. She had lost fifteen head. The trail of the rustlers petered out on hardpan west of Forked Spring.

As she lay in her bed unable to sleep, she found her thoughts turning to Eloise. What kind of a life would the girl have with Owney Devlin? She had seen Devlin briefly from a distance when he had come up to buy Tolliver's ranch last spring.

In the interim, he had acquired a partner, a man named Lassiter, so she had learned. The mention of the name turned her stomach cold. There were so many unsavory things she had heard about Lassiter. A gunman, a hired killer, it was whispered. What was Owney Devlin, who was about to marry a sweet young thing like Eloise Hartney, doing with such a man as Lassiter for a partner?

Before falling asleep, she resolved that she would confront Lassiter and let him know she would stand for no threats to K-27. She didn't worry too much about Devlin. Lassiter, however, was another matter.

In the morning when Hi Bishop and Stillway heard the boss tell her uncle that she intended to meet the Lassiter-Devlin herd, they exchanged glances.

Bishop laughed. "This'll be our chance. Kill Lassiter an' do it right in front of the boss."

"With her as a witness," Stillway put in, his scarred right cheek crinkling in a grin.

But when they saddled their horses and rode up to meet the boss, she wasn't too pleased about them accompanying her.

Her generous mouth tightened. "You two being along just might mean trouble."

"I heard plenty about this Lassiter hombre, Miss Kerrington," Bishop said, twisting his sombrero in his hands. His bald head gleamed in the early sun that filtered through cottonwoods beside the house. "You best let us go along. Me an' Tex won't let nothin' happen to you."

It was the wrong thing to say, which he knew the moment he opened his mouth.

"I can take care of myself, thank you." And she vaulted into the saddle and rode off.

With a jerk of his head, Hi Bishop took off after her, Stillway trailing along.

When she became aware they were following her, she reined in and sat waiting, her green eyes unfriendly. "I thought I told you two that . . ."

"Mr. Mike asked us to keep an eye on you," Bishop said with a smile. It was an outright lie about her uncle, but in the old man's senility he wouldn't remember not having said it.

"Oh, all right," she finally agreed. Then she gave a sharp warning. "But you two stay out of trouble."

"Yes, ma'am," Bishop said, flicking a guarded wink and a faint smile at Tex Stillway.

4

THAT MORNING OWNEY DEVLIN tried to appear casual as he sipped coffee at the dawn campfire and said he was thinking of riding on ahead. He wanted a look at the house in order to see how much work there was to do on it before he and Eloise moved in. "Then I figure to mosey on over to Wayfield an' see if by chance she's come in yet," he finished.

Lassiter, hunkered before the fire, cup in his hand, grinned at his partner who could hardly hold in his eagerness.

"Hell, I don't blame you for being anxious, Owney. I sure would be if I were in your shoes."

Devlin rubbed the side of his face thoughtfully. "But you wouldn't be in my shoes, would you? I mean you figure it's plumb foolishness for a man to send halfway across the country for a female he's never laid eyes on."

"Getting cold feet?" Lassiter joshed. He threw the dregs of lukewarm coffee into the fire and dropped his cup into the pan on the wagon's tailgate. The men were saddling up.

"Bet you are gettin' cold feet, Uncle Owney," Eddie Pyne piped up. Lassiter hadn't realized the kid was close enough to overhear. Eddie's wide grin was intended to show that it was all said in fun.

Devlin looked grim. "It is a mite of responsibility I'm takin' on. But I got to face up to it."

"It'll be painless," Lassiter said to make him feel good.

"All right with you if I take off?" Devlin asked, turning to Lassiter.

"Go on, get outa here. See you at the ranch." All Lassiter was hoping for was that Eloise would just show up. And not let his partner down.

Devlin rode north. He hated to pull out and leave the burden of throwing the herd onto new range to Lassiter. But Lassiter had read him correctly. He was anxious to see Eloise. And why not? he asked himself. All these weeks of waiting, the correspondence between them, the indecision. Then the glorious day when she wrote that she was accepting him.

Some miles north he began crossing land he at first had thought he would own by himself. But taking it on alone had proved too big a bite to comfortably chew. Thank God for Lassiter coming back into his life when he had. A man couldn't want a better partner.

When he looked at hills covered with good grass, his heart lifted. Not since early spring had he seen the place and only hoped it lived up to his expectations. It did. All but the house. The bunkhouse was in better shape than the main house, which hadn't been lived in since old Charlie Tolliver's wife died. After that he had bunked with his three-man crew. Gradually he sold off all his cattle; then realizing he had nothing left to sell but land, he looked around for a buyer.

Devlin had heard about it through a land speculator in Santa Fe.

Several times that morning he started for his horse and the ride to Wayfield, then something would catch his eye that needed fixing. And he'd putter for a spell. Finally he admitted to himself that he was actually afraid to ride to town and face up to the possibility that Eloise might be there. The other day he had been all fired up to meet her. Learning that she had not yet arrived produced a letdown such as he had never before experienced in his thirty-one years.

But he knew he had to get hold of himself. He had a fine partner in Lassiter and he was going to make a life for Eddie. Damn it, the kid deserved the best and Devlin intended he should have it. For he could never escape the gnawing guilt that if he hadn't been passed-out drunk, his sister, Eddie's mother, would be alive. He would never have allowed her no-good husband to hitch up a half-broke team to a spring wagon for the drive home.

At first, when planning to raise Eddie, he had figured on Eloise being a mother to him. But seeing Eddie in person after a lapse of some years, having lost track of time in the interim, he figured Eloise would be more of a companion to the kid than a mother. Near as he could tell, they were about the same age, give or take a year or two. . . .

A few minutes after Devlin had ridden off, Lassiter was just saddling up when he heard a woman's scream. It came from a great clump of oaks beyond the camp. The four riders—O'Hale, Upshaw, Burns and Hannigan—looked around, their faces tight as Lassiter, gun drawn, went loping on long legs toward the sound of the trouble.

When he burst through the trees, he saw Ruthie standing beside a pail of water, a damp rag on the ground at her feet. Her blouse was unbuttoned, the sleeves pushed up. He could see a bruise mark on her upper right arm.

Her pale eyes were frightened for a moment when she saw the gun and the look on his dark face.

"What happened?" he demanded.

"Something frightened me. A big jack rabbit, I think," she said with an attempted easy smile. But he could see tension at her lips.

Beyond the oaks where brush was thick, movement caught his eye. Presently, Eddie Pyne strolled into view, hands in his pockets.

Flashing Lassiter a defiant look, he said, "Somethin' happen here?"

"You're to stay away from Ruthie. I told you that."

"Hell, I come on her back here, her half naked. Wanted a kiss. Nothin' wrong with that." He glared at Lassiter.

"You don't hear very good, Eddie," Lassiter said ominously. "I told you to stay away. . . ."

"She's an easy woman. Anybody can tell that . . ."

Lassiter's hand flashed out, catching the younger man on the side of the face, knocking him backwards in a sprawl. "You're not to judge her or anybody else, Eddie."

It took Eddie Pyne only a moment to recover from the blow. Then with a bellow of rage he leaped to his feet and made a grab for his gun. But Lassiter seized his arm, took the weapon away and tossed it far into the brush. Eddie wasn't through. He came roaring in, arms flailing. Lassiter sidestepped and pinned his arms to his sides.

"Simmer down, Eddie, simmer down."

The crew came pounding up to stare. Old Tom Hefter yelled at the kid. "You was wrong, Eddie. Dammit, the gal deserves some privacy!"

At last the fight went out of Eddie Pyne. Lassiter turned him loose.

"You all right now?" Lassiter asked Ruthie.

"I'm sorry I caused trouble."

He gave her a pat on the arm. Eddie was searching the brush for his gun, his sweated face twisted in anger. Lassiter located the gun. After unloading it, he handed it over. Eddie snatched the weapon and jammed it into his holster.

Lassiter looked deep into the sullen eyes. "Don't figure to do anything foolish with that gun," he warned.

Eddie swallowed hard under the impact of Lassiter's cold-steel eyes. He turned away, possibly reflecting on his narrow escape. A beating or worse.

Ruthie caught Lassiter alone. "You have been so kind to me, not telling the others what I am. Or was, rather."

"We've all got things we'd like to forget."

Later on Lassiter was riding point when thin streamers of dust angling in from the northeast caught his eye. He drew his rifle, waiting until three riders materialized. One of them was an attractive woman in a shirt and Levis, a flat-crowned hat dangling from a chin strap. With her were two hard-eyed riders.

"Hello," she called. "I'm Allie Kerrington!"

With that he returned the rifle to its saddle scabbard.

She sat in her saddle, one well-formed hand fisted at her saddlehorn, green eyes searching his face. Cattle streamed past them.

"Let me guess," she said. "You're the man they call Lassiter."

"I am," he said with a nod.

There was nothing to read on her pretty face. As she turned in the saddle, her breasts stirred provocatively under the green shirt. "Is Owney Devlin here?" she asked.

Lassiter told her that Devlin had gone ahead to the house. He noticed her two riders exchange glances. The one with the scarred cheek gave his companion a faint smile, which put Lassiter on his guard.

"I wanted to talk something over with you both," Allie said.

"You can tell me and I'll pass the word on to Devlin."

She drew a deep breath that caused his gaze to drop again to her bosom. Her eyes narrowed. She wrapped her reins around the saddlehorn and folded her arms.

"It concerns Joe Rudd and his so-called pool," she said.

"I've met Rudd."

"And he wants you on his side and against the Kerringtons," she guessed.

Lassiter's reply was a shrug. He couldn't decide

whether he liked her or not. He thought he detected a certain arrogance in her voice when she mentioned Kerringtons.

She spoke of Rudd's tactics, how the Kerrington K-27 was nearly surrounded by pool members. "If you go in with him," she said levelly, "the circle will be complete."

"You're fretting needlessly, Miss Kerrington—"

"A little deeper than mere fretting, Mr. Lassiter," she interrupted coldly.

"I don't think we'll be joining Rudd's little club."

He spoke so quietly that she didn't believe she heard him correctly. He repeated it. Her arms dropped to her sides and she slumped momentarily in the saddle while watching him. Then her back straightened.

"Well, that certainly is good news. Does Mr. Devlin agree?"

At that moment, Eddie Pyne pushed through the brush on a buckskin, his arrogant young face lighted with pleasure at the sight of Allie. "I hear my uncle's name mentioned?"

"You're Devlin's nephew?" Allie asked.

"Eddie, we're having a business discussion," Lassiter said. "Get back with the herd so they don't drift."

Eddie's face flushed and he said, "Yes, sir, boss, sir."

Turning his horse, he rode to the tail end of the herd and began driving stragglers out of the brush.

"You two don't like each other much," Allie observed.

"He'll get over it," Lassiter replied. Or I'll get his uncle to buy out my share of the ranch and be on my way, Lassiter thought to himself. However, it was turning over in his mind so chillingly that he wasn't quite set when the scar-faced Kerrington rider suddenly rammed in his spurs, sending his horse almost broadside into Allie Kerrington's mount.

"Watch it, Miss Kerrington!" Tex Stillway yelled. "Lassiter's pullin' a gun!"

A weapon exploded, and Lassiter felt a twitch at his shirt sleeve. Spinning his horse, he saw the second man, bent over in the saddle, ready for another shot.

Allie Kerrington screamed, "Bishop . . . *don't!*"

Hi Bishop's second shot whipped toward a bank of threatening clouds, for Lassiter's .44 was in hand, firing. Hi Bishop's right shoulder abruptly sagged. He uttered a cry of pain. And his gun slipped from a hand suddenly wet with blood. By then his horse was bounding away with him hunched over in the saddle, arm flopping. At each leap of the horse a scream of pain broke from Bishop's lips.

Tex Stillway, in the few seconds since crashing into Allie Kerrington's horse, tried to fire pointblank at Lassiter. But again Lassiter's weapon spoke first. Stillway tumbled into the dust, one foot caught in his stirrup. As the horse started to run, Lassiter reached out a long arm and checked it.

Making sure that Bishop was still riding hard to get away and presenting no further threat, Lassiter dismounted. He pulled Stillway's foot from the stirrup and leaned down to stare at the scarred face.

Allie rode up and spoke in hushed tones. "He's dead, isn't he?"

Lassiter looked at her. "He is, ma'am."

Then there was a great crashing in the brush. His DL riders, led by Eddie Pyne, came roaring back.

Lassiter gestured angrily. *"Stay with the herd!"*

He knew well that the gunshots might cause a belated stampede among animals, which were so worn out after the long trek from New Mexico, so edgy that a sneeze could set them off.

"You all right, boss?" O'Hale yelled. Lassiter gestured that he was all right. They took one look at the dead man, flicked a glance at an ashen-faced Allie Kerrington, then galloped back to the herd.

When Allie found Lassiter's eyes on her, she lifted her chin and said, "I certainly hope you don't think I had anything to do with that attempt on your life."

"At this point I don't quite know what to think," he said as she leaned over her saddlehorn, her face grim as she watched him hoist Stillway over the back of his horse and tie the body in place.

"I'll tell the sheriff what happened," she said and rode away. When he had mounted he could see her in the distance, heading east, her horse at a lope.

Lassiter, leading Stillway's horse with its dangling burden, caught up with the wagon. "Tom, I could use a shot of that whiskey."

Hefter slowed the team and handed over the bottle. Ruthie, sharing the seat, seemed pale and shaken. "What in the world happened . . .?" her voice trailing away as she saw the dead man.

"Tom, near as I can figure it, we're almost to our boundaries," Lassiter said, handing back the bottle. "Go a few more miles, then let the herd spread out. You'll boss the job. I'll pass the word to the crew."

"Where'll you be goin'?" the old man wanted to know.

"I've got a dead man to deliver to the sheriff."

Riding on up to the herd, strung out for nearly half a mile, he passed the word about Hefter being boss in his absence.

When it came Eddie Pyne's turn to hear the news, his face flamed and sparks of indignation leaped in the eyes. "I'm Devlin's nephew," he said savagely, "so by rights I oughta be boss when neither one of you is around."

Lassiter rode away without even bothering to reply.

5

AFTER THE NOON MEAL, Eloise took a walk from one end of the main street to the other. It was a beautiful day, most of the sky a deep blue except for some rather angry-looking clouds to the north. Walking helped ease the tension in her body and cleared her mind. The longer the delay in meeting her future husband, the greater her anxiety. As she reached the west end of town and started back, she noticed many faces peering at her from the windows of a place called the Four Aces. It dawned on her suddenly that perhaps ladies weren't supposed to walk alone in a strange town. She wished Allie Kerrington was here to offer advice.

When she made the return trip and neared the Four Aces for a second time, she did see Mike Kerrington, Allie's uncle. He was wearing a loosely fitting black suit and a beaver hat. His weight was supported by two canes. He was so emaciated it seemed that a good puff of wind could blow him away. Although they hadn't been formally introduced, Eloise had seen him with Allie at a distance. She spoke to him pleasantly.

He leered at her and said, "If you're a new girl in town, you better keep south of Aster Street. Sheriff McBride don't like it. . . ."

She hurried on, not quite sure what he had meant. But her cheeks were flaming.

She returned to her chair on the hotel veranda, her heart pounding. That vicious old man. Oh, Owney Devlin, where are you? she wailed silently and peered both ways along the empty street as if hoping he might ride in.

It was later that she leaned forward in her chair and looked along the street again. But this time the only sign of movement was a man coming into town, leading a pack horse. A tall, dark, scowling man, she noted. As he passed the Four Aces, she saw men dart out into the street, pointing at the rider and the burden on his pack animal.

She saw him stop before a small building with a sign: SHERIFF'S OFFICE.

Curious, she went up the walk to see what all the excitement was about. By the time she got there, a crowd had materialized from nowhere. She heard somebody say something about a K-27 man. Wasn't that the Kerrington brand?

Some men, noting her approach, made a lane for her, removing their hats when they saw that she obviously was a lady.

"What in the world is happening?" she asked a wizened little man.

"Why, ma'am, it's Tex Stillway. Caught lead poisonin' he did. Knowed he would sooner or later."

"Lead poisoning. My, my," Eloise murmured sympathetically.

And then as those behind began to push and shove she found herself moved right up to the tall, dark man who was sawing through the ropes on his pack horse with a knife. At last his burden came free and he let it flop to the boardwalk.

She stared down open-mouthed at a man with a scarred cheek, the eyes wide open and coated with dust. The front of his shirt was bloodied. It was the first dead man she had ever seen. She turned cold.

It began with little jerky sobs that caused men to turn and stare at her. And then it became a screech, a terrible sound in Wayfield on what up to then had been a reasonably pleasant afternoon.

She screamed and ran back to the hotel.

Lassiter barely gave her a glance. He was facing a corpulent man wearing a badge who had been roused from his siesta by the babble of voices and the screams of the hysterical female. He stepped from his office, rubbing his eyes.

"Who you got there?" he managed to ask and toed the body with his boot. "By gad, it's Tex Stillway." He darted a suspicious glance at Lassiter. "How'd it happen?"

Lassiter explained. Then he said, "Miss Kerrington saw the whole thing. She can tell it straight. If she's a mind to, that is."

"What you mean?" Sheriff Vince McBride bellowed, "If she's a mind to?"

"I don't really know which side of the fence the lady's on."

The sounds of a woman's sobs came from the hotel.

"Who's that screechin' female?" Sheriff McBride wondered aloud.

"Goin' to marry with Owney Devlin," a man spoke up. "So she's been claimin'."

Lassiter looked in the direction of the hotel. And at that moment Owney Devlin rode into town.

His head bowed as if bearing a sizable burden, Devlin was oblivious to the crowd. Then he was aware of Lassiter running into the street, with everyone looking on.

"Owney, wait up!" Lassiter called. Quickly he described the trouble with Bishop and Stillway and the reaction of a certain young lady at the sight of a dead man.

"I'm sorry, Owney. I didn't know she was your Eloise. She's pretty upset. You better go and take care of her, Owney."

"Oh, Jesus," Devlin groaned and walked toward the hotel like a man going to the gallows.

Lassiter tied Devlin's horse to a hitching rail.

Sheriff McBride, an elk-horn toothpick slanted from thin lips, shook his head. "Two Kerrington men are tryin' to kill you." McBride gave a deep sigh. "Sounds like you bought mucho trouble along with Charlie Tolliver's ranch."

The angry voice of an older man suddenly interrupted the sheriff. "That's one of my riders!"

It was Mike Kerrington, thumping along on his two canes. Some men parted so he had a full view of Tex Stillway sprawled on the boardwalk. His blood was staining the planks.

"I demand an explanation, McBride!" Kerrington thundered.

Lassiter studied Kerrington, a man at one time six feet of bone and muscle, able to strut and bellow and get away with it. Now the voice as well as the man was diminished, a travesty.

"He tried to kill me," Lassiter said before the sheriff could open his mouth. "I was lucky."

"Sir, you are a damned liar!"

"Careful now, Mike," Vince McBride cautioned worriedly. But Kerrington ignored the sheriff.

"Who are you, sir?" he demanded of Lassiter.

"Lassiter."

Kerrington's wrinkled mouth twisted. "I've heard of you. Nothing good, I might add!"

Lassiter accepted the judgment with a straight face and started to turn away. But Mike Kerrington let one of his canes fall to the walk where it clattered. And at the same time he made an awkward attempt to draw a gun from under his coat. Lassiter caught the move from a corner of his eye.

Moving swiftly, Lassiter grabbed the arm, twisted it and a .45 came free in his hand. This he passed over to the sheriff, who accepted the weapon reluctantly.

"Keep it, Sheriff. Before he shoots himself."

In his humiliation, Kerrington began to scream oaths. But everyone ignored him. At the sheriff's request, two men picked up Stillway's body and carried it down an alley behind the sheriff's office and toward Wayfield Furniture Store and Undertakers.

"I'll see what Allie Kerrington's got to say about the shootin', Lassiter," McBride said, tucking his toothpick carefully into a pocket of his checkered vest.

"Tell Devlin I've gone to the ranch." Lassiter

started riding in that direction as the heads of speculating onlookers swiveled to watch him.

In the Wayfield House, Devlin's persistent knocking finally unlocked a door with peeling varnish to reveal a tearful Eloise Hartney.

"Eloise, I'm . . . I'm Owney Devlin. . . ." He was standing with his hat in nervous hands, swallowing, unable to meet her swollen eyes. "Sorry you had to see the dead man. . . ."

"It was the most . . . absolutely the most horrible thing I ever saw in my life," she was finally able to get out.

Devlin gestured at the room where there was a bed and chair and chest of drawers. Her open trunk was in a corner. "Can I come in so we can talk?"

"You most certainly may not. I imagine tongues are wagging enough as it is." Her voice shook and she wiped her eyes on a sodden handkerchief trimmed in blue lace.

They went to the lobby where other guests, most of them regulars at the hotel, pretended they weren't listening. Eloise sank to a chair, looking exhausted.

Trying to keep his voice down, Devlin explained the shooting as told to him so briefly by Lassiter. "They tried to murder Lassiter an' he killed that fella in self-defense."

"But you only have your partner's word for what happened."

"I trust Lassiter, ma'am, I mean, Eloise."

"But why would two men want to kill him?"

"I honestly don't know. But we'll find out in time, I reckon." Ever since it was about to actually take place, he had been dreading the meeting with Eloise Hartney. But to have it compounded by the tragedy of Stillway was almost too much. He groped for adequate words, explaining that sometimes in the West there was no way to understand sudden acts of violence.

She was still pale, obviously shaken from her experience of suddenly seeing a dead man. Her hands were clenched in the lap of her wrinkled dress. "I . . . I hope you're not cut from the same cloth as that man Lassiter," she said, shaking her head.

Devlin was all twisted up inside, sweating. If anything, Eloise was even prettier than her picture in the marriage catalogue, and there was a sweetness about her that tore at him. How he wished Lassiter were here to speak for him. Lassiter had a way of putting things, especially with the ladies. But somebody had said that Lassiter had gone to DL ranch.

"I . . . am dreadfully afraid that I have made a terrible mistake," Eloise said, putting a hand to her eyes. "I should never have left St. Louis."

"Don't *say* that . . . please don't say that." If others had not been watching in the cramped lobby, pretending not to, he would have gotten down on one knee to plead his case.

For five minutes, Devlin talked in low, urgent tones, telling her how pleased he was by her looks and her manner. How sorry he was that she had been exposed to the violent side of the West.

"Please don't go back to St. Louis," he finished. She had been special to him when their courtship was being conducted via the mail. But now that she was within touching distance, she was the most important thing in his life—even more important than starting up the new spread or raising his dead sister's boy and making a man of him.

"Things out at the ranch are kind of messy," Devlin explained when Eloise seemed to have calmed down. At least she no longer broke into spasms of weeping. "What I mean to say is that I wouldn't want you to come out there till I get things fixed up proper. You understand?"

She gave a slight bob of her head. A tendril of yellow hair had drifted down to curve against her tear-stained cheek. He longed to reach out and tuck it behind her soft ear, just to feel it between his fingers. When he thought of snuggling with her in a bed, his body almost burst with the pressure of his passion.

"Tell you what." Leaning over in his chair, his wide face twisted in what he hoped was a pleasant look, he suggested she stay on at the hotel for a week or so. "I'll send in my nephew to kinda look after you. He's a nice kid, kinda cocky, maybe, but he'll bust a gut doin' whatever you ask him. Besides, I want you two to get to know each other real good. What I mean to say is, I want you to be good friends."

"All right, Mr. Devlin," she finally said in a small voice.

"Couldn't you call me Owney?"

"Yes, Owney." She gave him a wistful smile that made a mountain of his heart. "I think I'll go to my room and lie down."

Thoughts of her stretched out on a bed took his breath away. "I . . . I'll see about a preacher marryin' us."

At her door, he tried to take her into his arms but she stepped back. However, she did lean forward, lips puckered, eyes squeezed shut. He kissed her resisting mouth.

"Got to figure some way to build a fire under you," he said awkwardly with a laugh.

Before leaving town, Devlin learned from Cavendish at the Four Aces that a traveling preacher was due in Wayfield within the week. Devlin headed for home, his heart reasonably light.

At the ranch he got Lassiter aside and told him that Eloise was even better-looking than he had anticipated. "She's about the purtiest damn female on this here globe."

Lassiter smiled at Devlin's enthusiasm. But the smile faded when Devlin revealed his plan to send his nephew to watch over Eloise Hartney in town.

After the herd was spread out, they went to work with hammer and saw and paintbrush. Doors in the house were rehung, windows repaired. Places where the flooring had buckled were nailed down.

They were in the midst of it when Allie Kerrington rode over with her foreman, Davey Prince. He was an older, tired-looking man who had worked for her father. Lassiter introduced them to Devlin.

"Pleased to meet ya, Miss Kerrington," Devlin boomed, keeping his paint-smeared hands out of reach.

When Devlin excused himself to resume painting a door, Allie walked with Lassiter out to the corral. Posts had been replaced, with new rails put in place.

"I want you to know, Lassiter, that I told the sheriff exactly what happened the other day. I don't know what got into Bishop and Stillway, but they definitely tried to kill you. Needless to say, I fired Bishop."

Lassiter thanked her for telling it straight to the sheriff.

"Did you think I might do otherwise, Lassiter?" she asked with a faint smile.

"After you rode off, I didn't know what to expect." His eyes were glinting. "But I do now."

That seemed to please her. She gestured at the barn, the house, the bunkhouse set back in some cottonwoods. "If things don't work out for you here, I'd like you to think about coming in with me." She stood tall, idly flipping a quirt against her boot top.

"What makes you think they wouldn't work out?" he asked bluntly.

She twisted a lock of auburn hair around a finger for a moment and looked thoughtful. "Oh, your partner with a new wife, for one thing."

"I knew what I was getting into from the first, Miss Kerrington," Lassiter said, which wasn't altogether true.

"I'd prefer you to call me Allie."

"All right, Allie."

She broke into a beautiful smile. "I like the way you say my name." That seemed to embarrass her, as if suddenly realizing she had gone too far. "I do want to say that the other day when Bishop and Stillway moved first, I never saw anyone react so fast as you did. It was incredible."

"Instinct, I guess," he said modestly.

"Davey is getting a little old and I do need a tough man to take over. Think about it, Lassiter. You'd be most welcome at K-27."

"Tell me, where did you get the twenty-seven in your brand?"

"It was my father's age when he started the ranch. He thought it would bring him luck. And it did. For a long time." Her eyes roved over his tall figure. "My father was a tough man like you, Lassiter. Tough but kind underneath. As I suspect you are."

"Maybe."

"I *know*." She gave a little laugh. Her eyes, bright with promise, lingered on his. Then with a wave of her hand she mounted up. He shook hands with Davey Prince and the two of them rode away.

Lassiter thought about the offer she had made. Then he dismissed it from his mind. Things would work out at DL. They had to, damn it!

Scowling, he picked up a hammer and strode into the house.

6

ELOISE FOUND THAT SOME of her fear of this untamed land was beginning to fade because of the soothing presence of Eddie Pyne. That first day he rode to town in the DL wagon and had the hotel fix up a picnic basket. She was overwhelmed by his thoughtfulness but a little fearful of what people might say. But he reassured her with a cocky grin, insisting that his mission at present was to make her happy—on orders of her future husband, Owney Devlin. They both laughed.

It was a beautiful day and Eddie was most considerate. He spread a blanket out for their picnic, first removing all stones and smoothing out rough spots on the ground with his boot. They feasted on cold chicken.

"Tomorrow I'll bring a bottle of wine," he said with a grin.

"We shouldn't do this so often, Eddie." But her heart was pounding strangely. When he kissed her, just a brief fluttering of his lips on hers, she felt as if a hot wire had suddenly been drawn through her body.

But they had another picnic the next day and the day after that. On the fourth day, she drank too much of the wine in the hot sun.

Her head swimming, she lay back, Eddie casting a shadow above her. She felt his fingers skip lightly over her breasts.

"Eddie . . . don't . . ." Her voice shook and was weak.

Then he was touching her bare flesh and she shivered and gasped. She felt her skirts being lifted, the sun hot against her bare thighs at the tops of her stockings.

"Eddie . . . we shouldn't . . ."

Things were going slowly at DL ranch. But Devlin insisted he wanted everything right before bringing Eloise to live in the house.

Later in the week, Allie Kerrington rode over with her foreman, Davey Prince.

"I was in town and thought I'd drop by," Allie said. "It's on my way home."

Lassiter was beginning to get his landmarks and knew that DL certainly wasn't on her way to K-27. But he didn't say anything. Prince remarked on how well the work seemed to be coming along and went over to talk to some of the men.

Lassiter had the feeling that Allie had something on her mind. She kept glancing at Devlin, who was planing a door, cursing under his breath.

Finally she walked over and said, "How soon do you intend to marry Miss Hartney?"

Devlin looked up, blinking at the question. "Soon's I get this place fit for her to live in."

"It looks fine now, Owney," she said, with urgency in her voice. "If I were you, I'd go to town and marry her. *Today!*"

Devlin straightened up, a faint grin on his face. "I want things to be right for Eloise. Meantime Eddie's takin' good care of her."

"The preacher is in town. You should marry her. Don't let any more time pass . . ." Then she caught herself, looked around at Lassiter, blushed slightly and walked away.

Lassiter heard her murmur, "I almost said too much."

"What were you trying to tell my partner?" Lassiter asked as he trailed along to her horse.

"I shouldn't butt in. He's a grown man and certainly able to take care of himself." She looked down from her saddle. "Have you given any more thought to our discussion of the other day? About you becoming my foreman?"

"And I asked you a question about what you were trying to tell my partner."

But she acted as if she hadn't heard him. She gave him a nod, which jiggled her chin strap, then rode away with Davey Prince.

Lassiter announced that he was going to town. He got away before Devlin could ask questions.

After the long ride he found Eddie Pyne at the livery barn, hitching a team to the DL wagon. Lassiter called him over to the oversized wagon yard where they'd be alone. A scowling Eddie followed him.

"What you want, Lassiter?" he asked grumpily.

"Your Uncle Owney has built his life around you, Eddie."

"Why you tellin' me that?" All of a sudden Eddie seemed ill at ease.

"Don't you do anything to hurt him."

"Never figure to."

Lassiter peered deeply into Eddie Pyne's face. "Just remember what I said," was his final warning.

Then Eddie began to curse, piling epithets on Lassiter's shoulders. Finally, standing it as long as possible, Lassiter feinted with his right. Eddie dodged into Lassiter's left, which dumped him on the seat of his pants. Lassiter leaned down and hauled him to his feet. The eyes of the younger man were slightly crossed and he mechanically rubbed his jaw where the blow had landed.

"I won't take cussing from any man," Lassiter said through his teeth. "Only because of your uncle I let you off easy."

The tone of Lassiter's voice seemed to drain away the last of Eddie Pyne's belligerence.

Later that week, after Lassiter had helped move cattle onto better grass, he dropped in at Apperson's, a trading post some twelve miles west of Wayfield. There was a general store, a saloon and cafe and some hotel rooms. He had heard that Ruthie was working there as a waitress and singer. When Lassiter walked in the door, her eyes sparkled at sight of him. She came running across the big barnlike place to hug him.

"Lassiter, Lassiter, it's so good to see you," she exclaimed. Several hard-eyed men drinking at the bar looked around but made no comment. She waited on him as he ate a hearty noonday meal and drank two bottles of beer.

When the place began to clear out, she came over
and sat at his table. Lassiter asked about the new job.

"It's just a way to make a little money so I can move
on," she said. "After Pete was killed I . . ." She looked
down at the table with its wet rings from the two
bottles of beer. "Pete had me under a tight rein. I
guess I'm not used to being on my own."

"How old are you, Ruthie?"

"Nineteen. The only life I've ever known was the
one Pete gave me."

"You can do better than this place."

She shrugged.

"What happened to your plan of going to Prescott?"
he asked.

"I thought I'd get a stake first."

They made small talk together. When Lassiter paid
for his meal and tipped her generously, her small face
was suddenly somber. "Maybe I shouldn't say anything, Lassiter, but you were good to me and I know
you're partners with Devlin . . ."

When she hesitated, seemingly embarrassed, Lassiter poked her arm with a long forefinger. "Tell me,
Ruthie."

"There's talk about Eddie Pyne and Devlin's intended," she blurted. "Teamsters coming through
here say that Eddie and the girl have picnics in lonely
places."

"Nothing wrong with that," Lassiter felt he should
say.

"A teamster I met told me that Eddie got fairly
drunk one night and . . . and he bragged."

"Kid talk, probably." Lassiter was uncomfortable.

"He's no kid. He's as old as I am."

"I've already warned him," Lassiter said heavily.

"And Devlin is so nice and all . . . but not very wise when it comes to women. At least that's the feeling I got when I was around him."

Ruthie followed him outside. Some men just mounting up under a big sign: APPERSON'S, lifted their hands to Ruthie. One of them said something under his breath and they all laughed. Ruthie blushed but kept her eyes on distant hills, looking so close on the clear afternoon that they could be touched.

When the riders had departed, Lassiter said, "If I gave you some money, where could you go, Ruthie?"

"I don't need any money," she said quickly. "I'm putting by a little each day. . . ."

"Apperson's isn't for you," he said.

She thought about it for a minute. "Let's just say it's a stop on the trail where I can take a few deep breaths and get over Pete. And then go on from there."

"Did you love him?"

"Oh, Lassiter, if you only knew." Tears glistened in her dark eyes. *"I hated him!"*

He tried to push two double eagles on her but she refused to take the twenty-dollar gold pieces. Lassiter finally gave up when she fisted both hands and kept backing up. He returned the coins to his pocket.

"Remember, if you need anything, let me know." He stood with one foot in the stirrup of his black. "Or if anybody insults you." He paused for emphasis. She knew what he meant, thinking of the riders and the one who had muttered something, causing them to laugh.

"I'll remember," she promised. But he wondered if she would.

7

At the door to her room, Eloise presented her cheek for Devlin to kiss. Then they marched together to the veranda, where they took chairs and sat stiffly. Thinking she was still upset about having Stillway's body practically thrust under her nose, Devlin tried again to explain. But she wasn't really listening. She watched two K-27 cowboys ride into town, hesitate in front of the Four Aces and then ride slowly to the far end of the block where they entered an establishment known as Matt's.

"You're still mighty cool to me, Eloise," Devlin said, twisting his hat in his lap. He was beginning to wonder again if sending for this bit of blond fluff, as Lassiter had once referred to her, had been a wise move. Was she never going to thaw?

Finally, what was bothering her spilled out. It was something entirely different from the matter of the dead Tex Stillway.

"I suppose it isn't unusual to travel with a camp woman," she said suddenly, "but I do think you could have gotten rid of her before everyone knew about it."

For a moment, Devlin was too surprised to open his mouth. Then he realized what she was getting at. "Where'd you hear that?" he demanded.

"One evening Mr. Rudd let it slip. He was very sorry about it afterward and told me to pay no attention. But the damage was done."

"Rudd, eh?" Something in Devlin's voice made Eloise look at him in surprise.

"Now don't go thinking things about Mr. Rudd. He's been a perfect gentleman."

"He damn well better be."

After a period of silence between them, Eloise said, "I see you're not going to explain about the camp woman. You intend to let me just go on . . . thinking things." Her voice began to shake. "I suppose she was passed from one to the other of you like a common . . ." Eloise clenched her small hands.

He began to tell her about Ruthie, how her husband had been killed in a runaway. He didn't know whether he believed the husband part of it, but it was Lassiter's story and he had decided from the first to accept it.

"Lassiter ordered the men to stay away from her," Devlin finished. "I hardly ever even laid eyes on her myself."

"Where is the woman now?"

"I hear she's workin' at a place out west of here. Apperson's it's called."

"Very well," Eloise said at last. "I'll accept your version of what happened. Mr. Rudd obviously has his facts wrong."

That pleased Devlin so much that he got up the nerve to suggest they go to the store and indulge in a sarsaparilla.

She gravely accepted his invitation. But while drinking daintily, she seemed so subdued that it worried him. He even asked if she was feeling well, and she assured him that she was.

But she didn't offer her cheek for him to kiss when he returned her to her door.

"Just about another week or so an' I'll have everything squared away out at the ranch," he said with a weak smile.

She only nodded and went into her room and closed the door.

Devlin hunted up Eddie and told him about Ruthie. "Try an' get her to understand how it was, will you, Eddie?"

Eddie nodded. "Eloise will pay attention to what I tell her."

"That's fine, Eddie, fine." He clapped his nephew on the back. "Stick it out for another week or so. Then it'll all be over."

Devlin noticed that Eddie got a pained look on his face for a moment. Then it vanished under a bright smile.

It was when Devlin happened to mention Lassiter's name that Eddie lost his smile and began to cuss.

"He came here to town an' practically accused me an' Eloise . . ." Eddie was too broken up to finish it.

A red-faced Devlin rode for home.

Lassiter was washing up in the pan on the bench beside the bunkhouse when Devlin rode in. Devlin came right to the point.

"Eddie hinted around that you accused him of . . . of . . . bad things with Eloise."

"I just want everything to go right for you, Owney."

"It ain't right to accuse Eddie. . . ."

"Oh, hell, Owney, that kid's been nothing but trouble since the day we left New Mexico."

There had been loud voices from the bunkhouse, men joshing after a hard day's work. But now there was silence. Listeners.

"Forget it, Owney," Lassiter said wearily. "I'm sorry. I apologize."

That seemed to take some of the steam out of Devlin. He leaned against the bunkhouse wall, shaking his head. "I admit Eddie's a little wild, but when me an' Eloise is married, she'll help to settle him down."

Lassiter regretted losing his temper. But he was so apprehensive that something would happen to spoil his partner's dream that it had just boiled over. "I wouldn't let any more grass grow before you marry her, though."

Devlin faced him, big and tough and red-faced. "There you go, thinkin' bad things about Eddie again."

"Leave the house as it is," Lassiter said as he had told him at least six times before. "Marry the girl. She'll more than likely put up with a lot more than a house that still needs fixing."

Devlin's mouth worked as he stared. Then his heavy shoulders sagged. "Maybe you're right, Lassiter. Just maybe you're right."

"Course I am!"

"All right, by gad. I'll marry her *tomorrow!*"

"That's good news," Lassiter said and grinned, giving his partner a hearty slap on the arm.

"First thing I'm gonna do is get me a bath at the barber shop," Devlin said and winked nervously.

"We'll be spendin' our honeymoon at the hotel an' I sure wanta smell nice."

"And I'll go have a drink while you're getting yourself prettied up," Lassiter laughed.

Devlin suddenly seemed ill at ease. "One thing I want you to understand, Lassiter. I'd like you to be my best man . . ."

"Glad to, Owney."

"But I figure I oughta let Eddie be it," Devlin said awkwardly. "It'll make him seem more like part of the family. You understand, Lassiter?"

"Of course."

Lassiter didn't much care one way or the other. He could understand Devlin's wanting the kid to act as his best man. It was about like the time they had decided on the letters of their names as their brand. They had flipped for it to see which letter would be first. Devlin had won. Lassiter took it in stride with a wry grin—as he now was accepting the news about Eddie.

They arrived in town later than planned. Because they would be some hours in town, they rode to the livery barn where their horses would be out of the sun for the rest of the day.

As they each gave the hostler a dollar, Devlin said, "Can you tell me where I can find the preacher?"

The lank hostler shifted a straw from one corner of his mouth to the other and pointed up the runway. A chunky man singing "Hail Moses," under his breath, was unhitching a team of horses from a buckboard.

"That's the Reverend Jakes up yonder," said the hostler as he started to unsaddle Devlin's mount.

"Come on, Lassiter," Devlin beckoned. "Let's have a word with the fella."

Lassiter trailed along. Devlin went up to Jakes and removed his hat. He hemmed and hawed for a moment while the bright-eyed reverend looked him over. "Want you to marry me," Devlin said, giving a nervous cackle of laughter. "About an hour from now."

"Who's the lucky lady?" the reverend asked as he loosened harness straps.

"Eloise Hartney."

Jakes stood with his back turned to Devlin. But Lassiter was in position to see his jaw drop and his face begin to lose color.

"S'posin' we meet at the hotel in one hour?" Devlin said grandly, his confidence now booming.

"F . . . fine," muttered Jakes.

"See you then, Reverend."

Outside in the bright sunlight, Devlin said, "Kind of a quiet cuss, ain't he?"

"Seems like it," Lassiter agreed and turned to look back into the livery barn. But he could see nothing because of the deep shadows.

Fifteen minutes later, Lassiter was standing at the bar in the Four Aces when he saw the reverend in his buckboard go pounding out the east road, using a whip on the team.

Lassiter was troubled. He ordered another drink, sipped it, waiting for Devlin. Presently, Joe Rudd and a huge man entered the saloon. Rudd introduced the man as Denver Quayle, mentioning that he was bareknuckle champ east of the Rockies and was here to work for him.

Then Rudd pointed at Lassiter standing down the bar and said loudly, "Denver, that's one of the partners I was tellin' you about."

Quayle, holding a glass, turned to look Lassiter over, eyes yellow and penetrating in a broad, scarred face. The saloon became very quiet, as the drinkers sensed sudden tension.

At that moment, Devlin, his face scrubbed clean, his hair freshly cut, came into the saloon. The big man, looking worried, came over to stand next to Lassiter.

"Owney, what's the matter?" Lassiter asked.

"I can't find Eloise anywheres," he moaned. "An' folks don't seem to want to talk about it."

"Reckon you'll have a long wait for her, Devlin," Rudd said with a malicious smile.

Devlin, in no mood for joshing at such a time, pushed away from the bar, his face reddening. "What'd you mean by that?" he demanded.

"I just said you'll have a long wait."

"You're a goddamned liar!" Devlin yelled. The long push from New Mexico, the added pressure of his nephew appearing suddenly and then Eloise's reaction to the sight of a dead man had ground down his nerve ends.

"I'll handle him, Rudd," Denver Quayle said in a gravelly voice. He set his glass down on the bar and pushed up his shirt sleeves over enormous forearms. He started purposefully across the sawdust strewn floor for Devlin. But Devlin stood his ground, face contorted, as if welcoming violence to ease the frustrations that had been boiling in him for so long.

Lassiter would have none of it; Devlin's wedding day wasn't to be spoiled—not by Quayle at any rate. Drawing his gun, Lassiter stepped between Devlin and the advancing Quayle. Men sucked in their breaths, shifted their feet, ready to run.

Quayle came up on his toes, stared at the cocked .44 pointed at his thick midriff. Then he lifted his eyes to Lassiter's face. "Step aside," he ordered.

"If it's your game . . . yours and Rudd's . . . to beat Devlin to a pulp, forget it."

Quayle took another tentative step, with everyone wide-eyed and pale. A nervous titter of excitement broke from someone in the gathering. All eyes were on the giant Denver Quayle, who seemed to have grown two sizes in the past few seconds. Lassiter stood implacable with the drawn gun gripped in a steady hand.

Quayle studied him for a moment, then the tension went out of his heavy shoulders. He started backing. To take the sting out of his retreat, he said ominously, "I'll remember this, Lassiter."

He stepped back to Rudd's side down the bar, picked up his glass and drank deeply. Only then did Lassiter holster his gun. A sigh of relief passed through the big room.

"Come on, Owney," he said in a low voice. "Let's go find your bride."

They hunted the town over; people were uncommunicative for the most part. They looked wherever Eloise might be: the dressmaker's, the store, the cafe.

Devlin began muttering to himself, his footsteps quickening almost to a trot as he moved toward the hotel once again. He saw Mike Kerrington just crossing the veranda, his two canes thumping.

Sight of the old man brought a joyous cry from Devlin. He turned to a grim Lassiter walking fast at his side. "That's it! Eloise has gone out to the Kerrington

70

ranch to spend the day with Allie . . . ain't that so, Mr. Kerrington!" Devlin shouted, and the old man paused at the top of the veranda steps, scowling in the direction of the voice. "My Eloise is out visitin' your niece, at the ranch."

The sight of Lassiter reminded Kerrington of being disarmed in front of half the town a few days before. His wrinkled lips drew tight against yellowed teeth.

"Ain't no such thing, Devlin!" he cried with a cackle of laughter. "Eloise Hartney an' your nephew was seen in a wagon goin' hellfire out the west road."

"That's a lie!" Devlin screamed.

Lassiter clamped strong fingers around Devlin's wrist. "Hold it in, Owney. That's twice inside half an hour you've called a man a liar."

"Reckon everybody else in town is scared to tell you," Mike Kerrington continued in a cackle of a voice.

The yelling brought several women in sunbonnets to the porch of the Wayfield Store. "I knowed no good would come of it," one of them said loud enough for Devlin to hear.

"I don't know this country very well, old man," Devlin said in a threatening voice as he advanced on Kerrington. "Whereabouts on the west road was they seen?"

"The road that goes by Apperson's," the old man said gleefully. "And eventually reaches Prescott. Reckon that's where they're headin'."

"There's some mistake," said Devlin, getting hold of himself. "Likely she's been taken ill an' Eddie is rushin' her to a hospital. . . . Oh, my God, poor Eloise!"

He whirled about and went loping for the livery stable. Lassiter was on his heels.

As they roared out of town, there was a lot of head shaking from those assembled to view the spectacle.

Rudd, standing at the front windows of the Four Aces with the rest of the customers, muttered, "The poor fool."

Rudd was talking to Denver Quayle when a timid voice spoke his name. Turning, Rudd saw Hi Bishop, a stained bandage on his right arm that was worn in a sling. Rudd's face tightened.

"Where the hell you been, Bishop?"

"Layin' low till my arm got better. Mr. Rudd, could I . . ." he glanced apprehensively at Denver Quayle hulking nearby. "Could I see you outside alone?" he finished.

Rudd smiled broadly. "Why sure, Hi. Just give me a minute to finish my drink. Be right with you."

After Hi Bishop had gone outside, moving to the left across the front of the saloon, Rudd jerked his head at Quayle.

"Just in case," he said, and Quayle followed him out.

They found Bishop in a slot between buildings in deep shadow. He looked nervously at Quayle who stayed up near the walk. Rudd came strolling along the slot, with his hands in his pockets, trailing cigar smoke.

"What'd you want to see me about, Hi?" he asked pleasantly.

Bishop shot a worried glance right and left, saw no

one within earshot save for Quayle, then lowered his voice. "I got fired from K-27. An' I need some money bad."

"You botched up that job I sent you on," Rudd reminded, no longer smiling. "You got Stillway killed and yourself shot up."

"That Lassiter . . . I never seen anybody move so fast in my life."

"You knew he was tough. Why didn't you keep your eyes open?"

"Hell, I did. But Stillway, he jumped the gun before I was set . . ."

"So now it's Stillway's fault."

"What I'm gettin' at is this. Next time I'll nail Lassiter good."

"You think there's gonna be a next time?" Clamping the cigar between strong teeth, Rudd suddenly seized Bishop by his bandaged arm. He tore at the bandages.

"Jeezus, what're you *doin'?*" Bishop cried.

"Just wanted to see if you've got any surprises wrapped up in those bandages. Such as a derringer."

"Not for you, Mr. Rudd. God no, not for you."

Rudd's lips twisted cruelly. "By rights I oughta pull that arm out of the socket."

Bishop backed up, losing color. "Gad, I'm hurtin' enough as it is!"

Rudd dug into his pocket and handed over a five-dollar gold piece. "Go up to Doc Hamilton's place. Have him put on a fresh bandage. You needed one anyhow."

Bishop dropped the gold piece into the pocket of his worn pants. "There'll be a next time for Lassiter?"

"We'll see."

Doc Hamilton, a plump, bald little man, accepted the money and went right to work. He had lived long enough on the Diablo range to know better than to ask questions.

When Rudd got back to the Four Aces, Sid Salone had just arrived. Rudd's dark little foreman had ridden in from the ranch.

Rudd told him what had happened, how Denver Quayle had been on his way to stomping Owney Devlin into the saloon floor when Lassiter had intervened with a gun.

"Quayle's got it in for Lassiter now," Rudd said with a smile. "For making him back down in front of everybody."

Then he told Salone about Eloise Hartney and chuckled.

When he had finished, Salone shook his head. "A damn foul trick for a man to do to his own uncle."

"Don't tell me that cold heart of yours is suddenly wrapped in compassion," Rudd said with a laugh.

Salone only shrugged a narrow shoulder and helped himself to Rudd's bottle. He saw Quayle enter the saloon. "That big bastard turns the back of my neck cold," Salone muttered.

The remark amused Rudd.

8

FOR THE FIRST FEW miles out of Wayfield, Lassiter kept yelling at Devlin to take it easy. But finally he gave up and kept his black at the same mad pace as Devlin's sweating buckskin. By the time they reached Apperson's, it was twilight.

"Our horses are done in," Lassiter yelled when Devlin barely slowed as they pounded across the big yard in front of the place. There were several wagons and saddlers off in the trees. As they came up to a nearly filled hitching rail, Lassiter, from a corner of his eye, glimpsed the DL wagon they had brought from New Mexico. The brand on the tailgate was plain to read in the fading light. His throat tightened and he wondered if Devlin had spotted it. He guessed not because Devlin was on the narrow porch, turning his head.

"You need a drink, Lassiter," he said and walked inside.

Had he seen the wagon, Lassiter reasoned, he would have other things on his mind.

Letting out a long-held breath, Lassiter followed him into Apperson's. Bill Apperson, a patch over one eye, overflowing a spindly chair, was pounding away at an old piano.

Several couples were dancing. Lassiter saw Ruthie on the dance floor with a tall young cowhand. At the sight of him, her face brightened. Then she saw Devlin and the brightness faded to a look of worry.

"What're you two doing way over here?" she asked with a strained smile.

"Huntin' for my nephew Eddie . . . an' . . . an' Eloise." It was hard for Devlin to get it out. "You see 'em, Ruthie?"

"No . . . no, I haven't." She looked at Lassiter and bit her lip.

"We need some food, Ruthie," Devlin said in a loud voice. "I'm so hungry I could eat a half-cooked mule."

Ruthie, hips swaying under a green dress, led the way to an empty table at the edge of the small dance floor.

"You wait on us, huh, Ruthie?" Devlin settled his bulk in a chair.

Ruthie looked embarrassed for a moment, then asked Apperson if it was all right if she waited on Devlin and Lassiter.

Apperson turned in his creaking chair and his fat face held a winking eye. "Give 'em anything they want."

He punctuated it with a howl of laughter and a chord hammered out on the piano, which brought rebel yells from some teamsters over in a corner.

"What time's the stage come through tomorrow, Ruthie?" Devlin asked, sitting tensely at the table. "I figure to head on over to Prescott."

"Stage doesn't come through till Thursday," Ruthie said a little nervously, with another guarded look at a grim Lassiter.

"Be damned," muttered Devlin, not seeming too disappointed about the coach. Then Devlin ordered for himself. "I want a steak as big as a wagon wheel an' a load of *frijoles* an' fried potatoes to go with it."

"How about you, Lassiter?" Ruthie asked, standing so close that he felt the pressure of her breast against his arm.

"Some of the same," Lassiter said with a forced smile.

When Ruthie started away to give the order to the cook, Devlin shouted after her. "An' bring a bottle an' two glasses!"

She gestured that she understood. The young cowhand who had been dancing with her stepped up and spoke to her earnestly. But she shook her head. He looked disappointed and walked away. Tobacco smoke curled into overhead lamps that were competing with the last of the daylight.

Apperson was banging on the piano again and couples were dancing. A pert little brunette in a short dress got Lassiter by the hand and tried to pull him to his feet. But he gave her a tight grin and shook his head.

Ruthie appeared with the bottle and glasses, her lithe body swaying in time to the music. She set them down on the table.

"Take one glass back, Ruthie," Lassiter said, shoving it toward her. She gave him a questioning look. But Devlin took the glass himself, picked up the bottle, worked out the cork with strong, yellowed teeth and poured generously into both glasses.

Lassiter leaned forward. Ruthie had gone back to the kitchen. "Owney, you've told me twenty times at least that you and whiskey don't mix too well."

"Hell, a man's got to have a drink on his weddin' day." Devlin tried to smile but it quickly died. And suddenly Lassiter sensed the truth.

Owney Devlin had also seen the DL wagon parked under the trees. Reaching down, Lassiter unobtrusively eased his .44 into its holster.

Ruthie brought platters of food. Devlin drank and ate voraciously. Lassiter suddenly had no appetite. He watched the whiskey he drank, the food he ate. It crossed his mind that a gunshot wound was compounded if the person shot had a full stomach. He had no idea what made that cross his mind. Only that Devlin was laughing too loudly, eating like a glutton and pouring a river of whiskey down his gullet. Devlin called for a second bottle.

"You've got to be sober enough to ride," Lassiter said when he managed to get Devlin's attention.

"Ride? Hell, we're spendin' the night here. Right here. . . ." Devlin was beginning to slur his words.

"I figure it's best if we head for DL," Lassiter said calmly, munching a forkful of greasy beans.

"We wouldn't git there till long past midnight," Devlin said, chewing.

"Won't matter. We'll sleep in tomorrow. Then Thursday you can catch the stage for Prescott. . . ."

Devlin's loud voice and his bellows of laughter were

beginning to worry Ruthie. It showed on her small face.

"Oh, Lassiter," she whispered once, leaning close.

But with a whoop, Devlin bounded from his chair, seized her around the waist and danced away with her. By then a fiddle player had joined Apperson at the piano. Devlin, with the slender Ruthie in his arms, pranced around the big room like a grizzly gone wild. Each thump of his heavy boots on the dance floor was accentuated by handclaps and shouts from onlookers.

When the music was finished, Devlin staggered over to the table, his clothing drenched with sweat, a wildness in his muddy brown eyes. Placing both hands on the table, he looked Lassiter full in the face. "I figure to go have a look at some of them bedrooms," he said.

Ruthie suddenly looked frightened and clutched at his arm. "Let's dance again, Owney!" she urged. He shook her away.

Then Devlin turned and staggered toward a dimly lighted hallway where the pert brunette was talking with one of the teamsters.

"Go after him, Lassiter," Ruthie said hoarsely. "At least get his gun."

Lassiter was already on his feet. He reached Devlin just as the latter was about to enter the hallway. Rows of doors were on either side, all of them closed.

Lassiter put out a big hand to tap Devlin on the shoulder. "Let's get outa this place, Owney."

"Why, sure," Devlin said. He smiled and turned around easily. Then he suddenly swung his fist, aiming for Lassiter's jaw. Lassiter jerked his head aside. Devlin's knuckles crashed against a door.

Devlin gave a bleat of pain and drew his gun. The

door was jerked open by a tall, thin man in long johns. Behind him an owl-eyed girl was peering out the door.

"What the hell," the man said, then saw Devlin's face and slammed the door shut and locked it.

"What room they in, Ruthie?" Devlin asked thinly, turning to the girl.

She stood as if transfixed, arms rigid at her sides.

"You keep out of it, Lassiter," Devlin spoke through his teeth.

"They're in . . . in number nine. The last room on this side," Ruthie gestured. And as Devlin staggered along the hall to the room indicated, she murmured, "Oh, my God!"

Lassiter was after him, with everybody crowding around the entrance to the hall in order to see the excitement. As Devlin reached the door, Lassiter was on him. He tried to get Devlin's gun. But Devlin broke free and rammed his heavy shoulder against the door. It burst open.

Coming to a sitting position on the bed were Eddie Pyle and Eloise. Eddie's face was the color of clabbered milk, hysteria building in his eyes.

Eloise was holding a blanket across her breasts. Her pale hair was loose, framing a pretty face tense with fear.

"Mr. Devlin!" she cried.

And Eddie wailed, "Uncle Owney, you gotta listen. . . ."

Devlin turned to Lassiter with a whoop of laughter. "Mr. Devlin, she calls me, by God. Me who sent her passage money an' money to feed her with." Suddenly he cocked the heavy pistol, his face ugly.

"Owney!" Lassiter yelled.

Devlin leaned over the foot of the bed and jerked away the blankets from the pair. In the lamplight spilling faintly from the hallway, they were both naked.

"You was *doin'* it!" Devlin cried with a bellow of bitter laughter.

Lassiter was edging forward, trying to get in a position to seize Devlin's gun hand. But he had to be so very careful. Any unnecessary jarring and the trigger mechanism would discharge.

Eloise was desperately trying to cover herself, but Devlin, catching her by an ankle, dragged her down the bed. She tried to hide her breasts with her forearms and cross her bare legs.

"Let 'em look!" Devlin yelled, waving his gun at the staring faces packed in the hallway. "Take a look, boys!"

"Uncle Owney!" Eddie screamed and made a frantic grab for a gun on the floor beside the bed. But Devlin, leaning over, gave him a backhanded punch with his free hand. The blow was so savage that it split his lips. Blood gushed. Eddie and Eloise screamed simultaneously.

Then Devlin's face was suddenly tight with fury. He aimed the gun at Eddie's groin.

Eddie cried out and tried to cover himself with his two fluttering hands. "Kill me, Uncle Owney, but don't shoot me . . . *there!*"

"Owney!" Lassiter yelled and tried to grab him.

"Uncle Owney," Eddie cried. "We're married. The preacher married us this morning! *We're man and wife!*"

Eloise burst into great gushing tears and flopped

over on her side, one rounded bare hip exposed. It had grown very quiet in the hall. Only Eloise's muffled sobs broke the stillness.

Finally, Devlin lowered his pistol. "Married, you say?"

"Yes, Uncle Owney! I've got the license. I'll show you. . . ." The kid was desperately reaching for his coat over the back of a chair. Blood dribbled down his chin, into his mouth, darkening the few chest hairs.

"I don't wanta see it," Devlin said in a suddenly dead voice. "Where was you headin' for?"

"Prescott," Eddie said in a shaking voice. At last he was able to get some of the blankets to cover Eloise and himself. "Then we was gonna take the steamer down the Colorado an' go back to St. Louis. We fell in love, Uncle Owney. I'm sorry. . . ." His voice trailed away. Tears mingled with the blood on his face.

"Ruthie, bring me ink an' pen an' paper," Devlin said.

She called for one of the other girls to do it, then stood with Devlin, an arm around his thick waist to steady him.

"Don't do anything foolish with that pen, Owney," Lassiter warned in a low voice.

When everything arrived, delivered by a plump girl in a red dress, Devlin brushed off Eddie's watch and some change from a chair seat onto the floor. Then, sitting on the bed, using the chair as a desk, he wrote out something quickly and signed his name. He dropped the paper on the bed, then got ponderously to his feet.

"That's a quit-claim deed to DL, Eddie my nephew," he said thinly.

While Eddie numbly stared at the paper, Lassiter said, "That's a damn fool thing to do, Owney." He reached out for it, but Eloise beat him to it, which caused Devlin to utter a hoot of laughter.

Eloise read it quickly, folded the paper and placed it under the blankets. With her wet eyes she stared defiantly first at Lassiter, then Devlin, then finally to those who crowded around the door.

"Eddie, you've got a new partner," Devlin said through his teeth. "Name of *Lassiter!* No me around to ease the way for you with him. Now you got Lassiter to deal with alone. Good luck."

Weaving, he made an about-face, with Ruthie still clinging to him. Those in the hallway made way for them and Lassiter.

They were back at the table, the big room strangely quiet now. Apperson was behind the bar, drinking, his eyepatch in place, his good eye on Devlin.

"You just can't give away your half of the ranch, Owney," Lassiter said earnestly.

"I never want to see the damn place again as long as I live." Then he pulled Ruthie onto his lap. "How about you an' me havin' a little of what I missed on what was s'posed to be my weddin' night?"

She looked at Lassiter, who said, "I'll be here to talk to him in the morning."

Ruthie looked across the room at Apperson. He nodded his head and she got up and walked away with Devlin. She did not look back at Lassiter but vanished from sight with the big, stumbling man at her side.

Lassiter drank too much and rented one of the rooms. He fell into a deep sleep and dreamed of a screaming Eloise and her new husband.

In the morning, Devlin refused to speak to Lassiter. Ruthie, looking glum, had brought the message.

But Lassiter ignored it and barged into the room that Devlin had shared with Ruthie for the night. Devlin sat on the edge of the bed, holding his head.

"Go on, say it, Lassiter. You warned me about Eddie an' I wouldn't listen. Now he's got DL to run along with you. I hope you ride his ass to hell an' back." Devlin spoke with such passion that spittle arced through the early sun slanting through the window.

"We've got to get hold of that quit-claim deed, Owney," Lassiter said calmly.

"You stay out of it, Lassiter. It's what I want. Eddie'll have to put up with *you!*"

"That's fool talk, Owney. You're giving away half a ranch."

"I don't want the damn place. Don't want to see it, ever!"

"We both worked hard for DL, damn it. Think of the hours we put in, the sweat."

Devlin raised his head. His skin was tight at the temples and his lips were twisted. Shadows were under his eyes that were sunken into his skull. He looked as if he'd been on a week-long drunk.

"You don't hear so good, Lassiter." Devlin's voice hardened. "I told you how I want it. Now get the hell out an' leave me alone!"

Lassiter hunted up Ruthie and asked about Eddie

and Eloise. She said they had left sometime in the night. She had no idea where they had gone.

She looked Lassiter in the eye. "I'll stay with Owney and try to see that he doesn't get in worse shape than he is."

"Yeah, I guess that's a good idea."

"I like Owney. He makes me feel like a lady." She nibbled at her lower lip. They were standing in front of Apperson's. The morning was cool and cottonwood leaves rustled in the breeze.

"I'll see if I can't get my hands on that quit-claim deed," Lassiter was saying. The last he had seen of it was Eloise putting it under the bedclothes.

"I need somebody to take care of, I guess." Ruthie looked wistful as she added, "I wish it was you. But I guess there's no chance, is there?" She waited a moment before speaking again. "No, I guess not, Lassiter."

"These days I've got too much on my mind," was the way he passed it off. He got on his horse. "You take care of Owney. I'll be back."

At DL, Tom Hefter had gotten hold of some Chinese lanterns, which he and the hands had strung in the trees by the front of the house. And across a wide front window someone had printed in soap: WELCOME TO THE NEWLYWEDS.

Lassiter looked at it and groaned.

9

ONE LOOK AT LASSITER'S face told the crew that something had gone sour. They crowded around, asking questions: Where was Devlin and his bride? Why hadn't they come back from town with Lassiter?

Deciding to get it over with, Lassiter bluntly revealed what had happened. He left out the part about Devlin finding Eddie and Eloise in bed together and the tragedy that had almost taken place.

"Eddie and the girl were thrown together in town and they just . . . fell in love, I guess, is the only way to put it," Lassiter said.

Even mentioning Eddie's name stirred up all of Lassiter's slumbering rage. "You might as well hear the rest of it. Devlin gave them his half of this ranch as a wedding present." That part was the hardest to get out. Tom Hefter and the hands stared at him with mouths open.

"I'll be holy damned," Hefter said, scrubbing a hand through his gray beard.

Eddie and Eloise arrived about an hour later. Eloise sat straight in the wagon seat, a faint breeze blowing tendrils of blond hair from under her bonnet. Eddie looked grim and apprehensive. When he saw Lassiter standing with legs spread, hands on hips, he lifted a hand. "Hello . . . partner!" He gave Lassiter a weak grin.

Eloise stepped from the wagon. Lassiter didn't offer her a hand. "Good morning, Mr. Lassiter," she said coolly and smoothed her skirts.

When Eddie drove the team and wagon down to the barn, Lassiter said, "What'd you do with that quit-claim deed?"

She had started for the house, but now she swung around, her gaze defiant. "I filed it at the courthouse."

Lassiter drew a deep breath. "So you're moving right in."

"Mr. Devlin gave us this chance and we're taking it."

"You're a slicker, Mrs. Pyne."

She looked vaguely startled for a moment, then said, "I'll have to get used to my new name."

"It should be Devlin. You know damn well it should."

"There's no need to swear, Mr. Lassiter."

He walked away before the temptation to slap her across her pretty face became overwhelming.

Two mornings later, Lassiter was taking the steam out of a big sorrel when Eloise came down from the house. She stood by the corral fence and watched him for a few minutes. When he came to a stop from cantering across the corral, to reach for the latch on the gate, she said, "Could I see you alone, Mr. Lassiter?"

She walked to the far side of the barn. Two of the men were mending harnesses. He didn't know where Eddie was. He didn't care. The news that Eloise had filed the quit-claim deed, making their hold on DL legal, had surprised him. He had been chewing it over these past two days.

"What do you want to talk about?" he asked gruffly.

"I just want you to know that I've never had anything in my life. Neither has Eddie," she said, putting the last in a little reluctantly, Lassiter thought. "I look on this partnership in the ranch as our one chance in life."

"So you said the other day."

"But I didn't say it very nicely." She turned so she could look up into his face. He noticed that her eyes glistened wetly in the early sun. He almost smiled; she was a good actress. "I just wanted you to understand, Lassiter," she continued.

"You went behind Owney Devlin's back," he said harshly, which caused her to color and lower her eyes. Then her head came up.

"Eddie and I didn't intend to fall in love. But we did. We were going to face up to him and tell him. But we . . . we . . . just panicked."

"You still could've faced up to him."

"By then all we could think about was getting away. Is Mr. Devlin going to be all right?"

"Why would you give a good goddamn?"

Lassiter's harshness caused her to burst into tears. She ran to the house. Presently, Eddie stalked out, wearing a ring of shaving soap on his face, which he had hastily tried to wipe off. He was wearing a gun.

Tom Hefter saw him from the bunkhouse and leaned out a window to warn Lassiter. "Eddie's acting like he's just sat on a scorpion. You better watch it, Lassiter."

Lassiter strode to meet him.

"What'd you say to my wife to make her cry?" Eddie demanded.

"You ever use that tone of voice on me again," Lassiter warned, leaning down so that his face was inches from Eddie's, "you'll find yourself on the seat of your pants."

Eddie swore and started to make a grab for his gun. But something in Lassiter's eyes arrested his hand. He stood for a minute, his right arm at an awkward angle. Then the arm fell to his side. Turning on his heel, he walked back to the house, much slower than when he had come out.

The following day Lassiter ran into Joe Rudd near the DL north boundary. With him was the tough little foreman Sid Salone and Denver Quayle. The latter rested a beefy forearm on the saddlehorn and tried to lock eyes with Lassiter, who took it for a time then grew tired of the game. Rudd, who noticed what was going on, let a small smile wander across his lips. Today he was wearing a black suit, his trousers shoved into polished boots. As usual he was armed.

"Too bad about you losing a partner," Rudd said, removing a cigarillo from a shirt pocket but not offering one to Lassiter.

"Devlin will be back at DL," Lassiter snapped and started to ride away.

"I guess you've heard about the fight."

Lassiter halted his horse. "What fight?"

"Devlin and Quayle. To be held at the Wayfield wagon yard."

"What kind of a game is this?" Lassiter demanded.

"No game. Devlin's willing. Purse of five thousand dollars. Should draw a crowd from fifty miles around."

Lassiter spurred his horse. He arrived at Apperson's tired and dusty. Devlin had been living in a shack with Ruthie out back of the place. Lassiter found him lifting a sandbag in the hot sun.

"What do you think you're doing, Owney?"

"Getting my muscles in shape. I s'pose you heard about the fight."

"Today I heard." Lassiter stepped down. "What the hell's it all about?"

Lassiter followed Devlin to some shade. "I haven't been drinkin'. An' Ruthie's been feedin' me good. I figure to take that big son of a bitch."

"You got no chance, Owney. I heard he's a bare-knuckle champ."

"We've cleaned out a few saloons in our time, Lassiter. You've seen me in action." Devlin chuckled and took a drink from a canteen.

"You're loco, Owney."

Devlin's face darkened. "It's my one chance. I'm takin' it." He rubbed his jaw. "I need the money."

"Good God, you've got DL. . . ."

"I give it away." Devlin's eyes were hard. "I don't want to talk about it!"

Devlin went back to hefting the sack of sand while Lassiter had a talk with Ruthie. The shack was neat and clean, the dirt floor freshly dampened and swept.

She tried a bright smile that didn't quite come off. "What's this crazy idea of Owney fighting Denver Quayle?" Lassiter demanded, straddling a chair.

"Joe Rudd made him the proposition. Owney is determined to go through with it. I think he can beat that Quayle. Owney is nearly as big—"

"What happens if Owney wins?" Lassiter interrupted.

"We'll use the money to go away. Mexico, Owney says."

Lassiter spent most of an hour trying to talk Devlin out of it, but the man was adamant. At last he gave up and rode home.

On the day of the fight, Lassiter rode to Wayfield. The town was jammed. Ruthie saw him and came at a run. He slipped off his horse and slung an arm around her waist. "What's happened?" he asked tensely, studying her drawn face.

"Owney got drunk last night. He's still drunk. He thinks he can fight that Denver Quayle. Quayle will kill him." It ended in a moan.

"Where's Owney now?"

"At the Four Aces." Lassiter glanced through the jam of buggies and wagons and saddles at the saloon building. There was a crowd of men in front.

Rudd came out of the hotel and saw Lassiter on the crowded boardwalk, his arm around Ruthie's slender waist.

"Sweethearts," he said with a smile. "Devlin won't like that. Being cut off from his women twice in a row."

Lassiter felt a nudge of temper.

Rudd said, "By the way, I happen to have a couple of tickets left for the big fight."

"You figure to get rich off this fight, I suppose," Lassiter said thinly.

"Not rich. Just make a few dollars." With a laugh, Rudd crossed the street, trailing cigar smoke.

"Wait'll he finds out Owney's drunk," Ruthie murmured with a shake of her head.

"I'll go fetch Owney," Lassiter said. "You get him home." Wherever the hell home was, Lassiter thought. Devlin had signed his away to nephew and wife. "If he's too drunk to set a saddle, we better hire a wagon."

"I think I can manage. Just get him away from Quayle. It's all I ask."

As Lassiter started to cross the crowded street toward the Four Aces, he heard a woman call his name. Turning his head, he saw Allie on the hotel veranda. "Could I see you a minute, Lassiter?"

"I'm kind of in a hurry . . . oh, all right."

He crossed the walk and stood looking up at her. She seemed on edge and he supposed it was because of his blunt manner. He could have been nicer about it, he told himself. He knew she had been under a strain because of the recent death of Mike Kerrington. "I'm really sorry about your uncle, Miss Kerrington."

"Thank you. I do miss him." She drew a deep breath, then said, "Now that your position at DL has changed, perhaps you'd consider being my foreman."

"Nothing's changed, Miss Kerrington. I've got a ranch to run."

She looked surprised. "But I thought . . ."

"You thought what?" he demanded suspiciously.

"Joe Rudd told me that he was buying out your half of DL. That he and Eddie Pyne were going to operate it together."

Lassiter gave a dry laugh. "You've been misinformed, Miss Kerrington."

"Oh, stop calling me Miss Kerrington!" She stamped her foot on the veranda flooring. A tear wandered across a curve of cheek, which she angrily brushed away. These days he was always making women weep, he thought. He was thinking of Eloise. Allie Kerrington leaned forward, gripping the veranda railing while peering down at him. "I thought that perhaps . . . just perhaps you'd have the courtesy to listen to me."

"If Rudd told you I was selling my share of DL, he lied. I'm staying put."

Before he could say another word, she stormed into the hotel. He could hear her running down the hall. Men were starting to drift toward the wagon yard behind the livery stable with its high board fence and solid gates. A perfect setting for a fight that undoubtedly would make northern Arizona history, someone said. Lassiter crossed the street.

Lassiter looked around the crowded Four Aces, spotted Owney Devlin slouched at a table, a foolish grin on his face. A half-filled bottle of whiskey was on the table. He held a glass in one large hand. Standing in front of him, thumbs hooked in vest pockets, was Joe Rudd. He had a black scowl on his face.

"You're yellow, Devlin," Rudd accused him in a shaking voice. "Got yourself drunk so you wouldn't have to face up to Denver Quayle."

"I can fight. . . ." Devlin's head bobbed.

"And after you pleading with me," Rudd continued in a nasty voice. " 'Oh, give me the fight, Rudd, I've got to earn some money.' " Faint laughter rolled through the tension-filled room because Rudd was mimicking Devlin's voice so realistically.

"I'll put his head under a hoss trough ten times," Quayle said in his heavy voice. "An' he'll be sober enough to fight me."

Quayle shouldered his way through the crowd and grabbed Devlin by the arm. He tried to pull Devlin out of the chair. But Devlin's body seemed to have suddenly developed a loss of bone; he was rag limp.

With a sound of disgust, Quayle let him fall back into the chair where he sagged, chin on his chest. "Got to get a better grip on him." Quayle started to put both hands on Devlin. Lassiter's voice crackled through the room. Every head jerked around.

"Leave him alone," Lassiter ordered.

Quayle looked back and gave Lassiter a speculative glance. Then he flicked his gaze to Joe Rudd who stood with Sid Salone at the jammed bar. From a corner of his eye, Lassiter thought he saw Rudd give a slight nod of his head, but he couldn't be sure. His attention was mostly on Quayle at the moment.

"Who you tellin' to leave who alone?" Quayle demanded sullenly, stepping back from Devlin. Men gave way.

"He's too drunk to fight," Lassiter said. "You'll kill him."

"Like I said, I'll sober him up."

"And like *I* said, stay away from him."

"I figured fightin' me would give Devlin a chance to get some of the cussedness outa his system—put there when he found his nephew an' that purty little gal who was livin' at the hotel in bed together out at Apperson's.''

This caused a stir, a ripple of whispers as those who hadn't heard the story got it in detail.

Lassiter cut Quayle's description of the incident short by brushing past the man and grabbing Devlin. "Come on, Owney, we're going home."

"I purely got no home." Devlin's head wagged and, with his rolled eyes, gave Lassiter a stupid look.

"Your home's at DL, quit-claim deed or not!"

Ed Cavendish, sensing trouble, came out from behind his bar, waving his hands frantically in the air, fear on his face framed by bushy sideburns. "Please, no trouble in my place. It took me most of a year to patch up from the last ruckus I had in here."

He was generally ignored as the crowd of drinkers grew quiet, those in the back standing on tiptoe. It seemed that every breath in the place was being held. Everyone was fascinated by the fact that Quayle was pushing his shirt sleeves up over his bulging forearms.

A grinning Quayle continued to rip into Devlin by talking about his nephew.

"Yeah, Eddie Pyne an' that Eloise havin' picnics most every day. They thought they was bein' smart about it but everybody knew what they was up to."

Lassiter debated; he had Devlin half out of the chair. But Quayle didn't let up. "It's a wonder they didn't get all sunburned takin' their clothes off out there in the open like that . . ."

Lassiter couldn't let this continue. For sure, Devlin was incapable of coping with the insults.

Lassiter allowed Devlin to slump back to the chair

where his upper body flopped over onto the table. Devlin, turned sideways, wore a foolish grin.

"Keep your mouth shut about Eddie Pyne and the young lady," Lassiter warned coldly. "They're married now and deserve respect."

"Amen to that," someone said from the back of the crowd.

Rudd looked irritated and tried to see who had spoken.

But Quayle was moving by then. Lassiter's drawn gun pulled him up short. "Enough," was Lassiter's crisp warning. In the crowd at the bar, he glimpsed Hi Bishop, arm in a sling, eyes murderous. A den of rattlesnakes I'm in, was the thought that streaked across Lassiter's mind.

"Somebody better go fetch the sheriff!" a man yelled.

"He's outa town," Rudd said with a tight grin. "Collecting back taxes." Rudd eyed Lassiter. "So don't expect McBride to be your wet nurse."

"If he's out of town, you sent him, I'll bet on that!"

Rudd laughed. "Put up your gun, Lassiter."

Lassiter still had it trained on Quayle, who said, "Killin' an unarmed man is a hangin' offense."

A few Rudd sympathizers agreed and waited to see what Lassiter's next move would be.

"I figure to get Devlin out of here." Lassiter had to raise his voice so he could be heard above the noisy crowd. "And don't anybody try and jump me!"

But when he reached for Devlin, the man slipped off his chair to the floor. He began to snore. There were titters of nervous laughter.

As Lassiter bent down to haul him to his feet, he

was suddenly aware of movement at his back. Twisting around, he glimpsed Sid Salone diving for his knees. Before he could turn aside and bring the barrel of his weapon down on the foreman's head, he was falling. He dropped his gun. Ed Cavendish snatched it up and stepped behind his bar. Lassiter had fallen heavily and rolled aside just as Quayle aimed a kick at his head.

This brought on shouts, mostly from Rudd's men and sympathizers: "Kill 'im, Quayle!"

Lassiter, on his haunches, lurched backward to avoid another vicious swing of a boot toe aimed at his skull. As he scrambled to his feet, Quayle hit him a glancing blow on the forehead. Even so, it had enough power to be felt at his knees. Staggering erect, he went after Quayle, landing lefts and rights to Quayle's midsection, the crowd of onlookers scurrying to get out of the way. Powerful as they were, the blows produced only a grunt from the big man.

Knowing he had to take the fight out into the street, to give him room, Lassiter backed to the doors. He tripped over an outstretched leg. As he started to fall, Quayle lunged, picked him up and threw him bodily through the swinging doors. Lassiter landed hard at the edge of the boardwalk and rolled into the street. It startled horses at the packed hitching posts.

Leaping to his feet, Lassiter struck Quayle a smashing blow to the face. But Denver Quayle only flashed a vicious smile and approached him.

10

IT WAS A TIME for brute strength; there was no time for science. Quayle was like an enraged bear, circling and roaring in, smashing his fists against flesh. When Lassiter backed up after delivering a flurry of blows to Quayle's face, the other man tried to kick him in the groin. But Lassiter drew back, seized Quayle's foot and twisted hard. Screeching with pain, Quayle danced about, trying desperately to reach the length of the extended leg and break Lassiter's hold.

With a final twist of the foot, Lassiter dumped him in the dust. But Lassiter did not try and pin the big man to the street. Quayle's powerful arms could snap his spine if he got in that close.

Breathing hard, Lassiter stood waiting. "Get on your feet if you want to finish it."

With the excited crowd watching, Quayle took a few precious moments to regain his breath. Suddenly he bounded to his feet, momentum flinging droplets of sweat into Lassiter's face. Quayle roared in, flailing wildly. Most of the time Lassiter was able to parry and give in return. But some sledgehammer blows got through. The punishment was severe. Lassiter felt blood running down the left side of his face. His ribs pained him where Quayle's heavy fists had pounded his flesh.

Aware that Quayle intended to kill him and that Sheriff McBride wouldn't lift a finger to stop it, Lassiter felt a growing desperation. They rushed together, clinched, arms wrapped around each other's torso. Quayle, who was taller, lifted Lassiter off the ground. But before Quayle could throw him down, Lassiter freed one arm and thumbed at Quayle's eyeball. With a yell, Quayle released his hold and jumped back, blinking.

Lassiter followed up with two savage blows to the jaw. A great yell exploded from onlookers as Lassiter struck again and again. Quayle was reeling. Joe Rudd wore a sour expression. The dark face of his foreman, Salone, was unreadable. When Hi Bishop got in close enough to thrust out a foot and trip the advancing Lassiter, Rudd's face beamed.

As Lassiter put out both hands to break his fall, Quayle bellowed his pleasure and rammed a kneecap into Lassiter's cheekbone.

Lightning exploded in Lassiter's skull. He fell flat. Looking up dazedly, he saw the dusty sole of Quayle's boot as it drew back. Quayle's intention was plain: to kick him in the head.

Dimly he heard a woman's voice. "Back off, Quayle! Give him a chance to reach his feet!"

Quayle bared his teeth. "Hell I will!"

"Not another step, Quayle!"

Finally the world quit spinning long enough so that

Lassiter was able to see Allie Kerrington in shirt and Levis pointing a revolver at Quayle. And it finally dawned on the big man, who snarled, "All right, Lassiter. Get up!"

Lassiter circled warily, seeing the bank of faces, hearing the yells. He saw Allie holster her revolver and step back to stand with arms folded. A look on her face indicated she was close to tears. But he couldn't reflect on it because Quayle smeared blood across his mouth with his forearm and rushed in. His intention was obviously to end it.

But Lassiter continued to circle, to parry, until his mind cleared completely. When he no longer saw three Quayles but only one, he began to pinpoint his blows—a left to the midriff, a right to the jaw—not always landing cleanly but with sufficient power so that Quayle's legs were soon trembling.

"Damn you!" Quayle screamed, bloodied and hurting.

But still he came on. Every ounce of his remaining strength it seemed went into a sudden roundhouse. Had it landed, Lassiter's head would have rolled. But Lassiter ducked just in time, came in under the whistling fists and landed two savage blows to the solar plexus.

Stale whiskey breath inundated Lassiter. He struck a second time and Quayle's right leg twitched and he almost went down. By then, Quayle had to tilt his head in order to see out of purpling eyes that were becoming mere slits. Lassiter, so tired he could hardly lift his arms, gamely met every lunge of the staggering giant. Quayle refused to go down. His reputation and pride were at stake. And he had no intention of being whipped by a smaller man before a roaring crowd.

Desperately, he plodded in, fists swinging. Lassiter backed up until his boots came up against the edge of the boardwalk. As he fell backward, men jumped aside to give him room.

"Get him, Lassiter!" one of them yelled and the cry was taken up by others.

Quayle flung himself down, pinning Lassiter. He felt a tremendous weight, smothered against one of Quayle's powerful shoulders. But before the bigger man could finish him, Lassiter cracked his right knee upward. It brushed the groin but was of sufficient power so that Quayle gave a yell and rolled aside.

Both men sprang to their feet at the same time. For an instant, Lassiter saw the solid jaw, flecked with blood, within striking distance. Skin had peeled away from Quayle's cheekbone. Blood had spilled across the front of his torn shirt.

Everything he had left went into that right smash to Quayle's jaw. Quayle's head jerked back under the impact but he didn't go down. Lassiter was dismayed. But then Quayle took a few staggering steps. His eyes crossed. His knees caved. He fell headlong into the street. For a moment, there was dead silence—then bedlam. The only silent ones were Rudd and the members of his pool.

Hands hammered Lassiter's back and arms. Well-wishers screeched their pleasure in his ears. They wanted to buy him all the whiskey he could drink. And he could have any girl he wanted at the *congal*. But he had something to do.

He pushed his way into the Four Aces. Cavendish stood white-faced in front of his bar. "I want my gun," Lassiter demanded. Cavendish gave it to him. Then Lassiter walked painfully to a table where Devlin was slumped, staring owlishly at the sawdust-strewn floor.

"Owney, get up," Lassiter urged. Seizing Devlin by an arm, he got him outside. Ruthie rode up then, her small face anxious, leading Devlin's horse.

"I'll take him home, Lassiter."

Lassiter nodded and as he watched them ride out, he saw a familiar figure in the crowd still swarming around him. He staggered across the street to lay a hand on Allie Kerrington's arm.

"Thanks for what you did," he said sincerely.

"You're a sight, do you know that?"

"I expect I am." It hurt to talk. He knew his front teeth had been loosened. He tried to grin and failed.

"Let me take you to my place," she whispered, leaning close, her eyes shining. "I'll take good care of you."

But Sheriff McBride had arrived back in town and insisted on hearing from Lassiter what had been going on in his absence. Lassiter told him while the crowd grew, hanging onto his every word as they relived the dramatic happenings of the afternoon.

By the time Lassiter was finished, he was so exhausted he got on his horse and started for home. He was out of town before remembering Allie Kerrington's warm invitation. He considered it briefly and looked over his shoulder to see if he could spot her. But there was no sign of her. He started riding for DL.

*　　*　　*

A frustrated Joe Rudd vowed to destroy anyone connected with Lassiter. Today he had planned to have Quayle finish off Owney Devlin. But Devlin had spoiled it by getting drunk. He was in a dark mood. After the fight, he noticed that the girl from Apperson's had shown compassion for Devlin and ridden off with him. What was it Eddie Pyne had told him in one of their talks about the girl? He'd have to remember and ask Eddie to repeat how they had met up with her on the trail from New Mexico.

Sid Salone sidled up to Rudd. "I didn't think Lassiter had it in him to handle Quayle like he done."

Rudd stood at the edge of the walk, thinking of Quayle being carried to the doctor's office across town. It had taken four men to handle the sagging weight of the bloodied and unconscious bare-knuckle champ.

"Quayle will never be able to hold his head up again," Rudd said angrily.

Hi Bishop worked his way through the crowd to Rudd's side. "I just seen Lassiter head outa town," he said in a low voice.

Rudd met Bishop's pale eyes, then let his gaze lower to the bandaged arm in the sling. "You didn't do so well last time," he reminded him, but Bishop smiled tensely.

"Is it still two hundred dollars?" he whispered.

Rudd gave a slight nod of his head. "Yeah."

"This time I won't have to split it with Tex." Bishop flashed a fierce grin.

"Just be careful this time, Hi," Rudd suggested, still in that low voice. "After it's over, spend your money down at Tucson."

"I'm practically on my way," Bishop said jauntily.

When Bishop was lost in the crowd that was beginning to disperse, Salone said, "You think he can handle Lassiter?"

"Maybe. I figure Lassiter's pretty well busted up."

Hi Bishop rode hard to get Lassiter in sight. Finally he saw a flag of dust ahead of him. He slowed his pace and saw Lassiter, who rode with his chin on his chest, right arm dangling. The reins were held in his left hand with apparently just enough pressure to keep the horse moving in a straight line. Lassiter's head bobbed at each step of the horse.

It was beginning to get dark. Flags of red hovered about the western horizon. Realizing he had precious few minutes of daylight left, Bishop looked ahead for a vantage point. A series of low hills studded with oaks caught his eye. He cut down into a canyon which he knew would bring him into the road about a mile ahead.

Tension set his wounded arm to throbbing. The palm of his right hand was moist and his heart pounded as he came out above the road. Minutes ticked away. No Lassiter. Although the twilight was cool, sweat stung Bishop's eyes. Leaning over in the saddle, he peered back down the road but could see no more than fifty yards because there was a bend in it.

He wanted that promised two hundred dollars and with night fast approaching, he'd have to make his move. Drawing his gun, he wrapped it in the bandages of his arm. He started back down the road, his horse at a walk.

The throbbing pain of his right hand had jerked Lassiter out of his semiconscious state. In the faint light, a creek sparkled ahead. He got stiffly from the saddle. He was thinking again of Allie Kerrington saying, "I'll take good care of you. . . ." There was something fascinating about her even though at times she did gall him.

When he knelt to drink at the creek, his right leg almost gave way. He had suffered a brutal kick from Quayle's hard boot. And worse than that, his right hand was swollen almost twice its normal size. He tried to draw his gun to see if it could be done. But his swollen fingers refused to fold themselves around the grip.

He suddenly heard the sounds of a horse coming at a walk. A thread of panic began to burgeon when he tried to get up and reach his rifle and his right leg buckled. He fell, halfway in the creek.

Somehow he pulled himself out of the water.

He heard a man laugh. When he tried again to reach his feet, the right leg refused to support his weight. He fell headlong. As he twisted aside, he desperately freed his gun with the left hand. And as he reached a sitting position, he felt a jarring of the ground near his hip. Then came the crash of the gun.

By then, he identified his assailant as the one who'd been wounded the day he had killed Tex Stillway. Hi Bishop had dismounted and was coming at a dog trot, his bad arm hugged tight against his body. But mingled with the bandages Lassiter made out the snout of a revolver.

"You're too damned lucky, Lassiter," Bishop said with a wild laugh as he came to a halt. "But not this time. You're so stove up you can't even grab your gun."

And then the awful truth struck Bishop like a blow. He was close enough now and the light was good enough for him to see that Lassiter's holster was empty. Too late he saw the gun in Lassiter's *left* hand. They fired simultaneously, or so it seemed. But Lassiter's gun hammer dropped a split second before Bishop's. The latter's bullet screamed into the oaks, shredding leaves. Bishop took a staggering step. He had lost his hat and his bald head glistened with sweat. In the shadows, it reminded Lassiter of a full moon. As Bishop started to lift his gun, Lassiter put a bullet into the moon. Bishop went down.

Diminishing gunshot echoes hammered between the hills as Lassiter painfully made his way to where Bishop was lying. He kicked the man's gun out of reach. But there was no need: Bishop was dead.

He decided to leave Bishop where he was and let somebody else figure out what had happened. He didn't feel up to unsaddling the man's horse. But he did tie the reins to the saddlehorn and swatted the animal so that it headed back down the road toward town.

Apperson's was one hell of a long way, he decided. And going to DL was no joy. So he backtracked.

At last he was in front of Allie Kerrington's ranch house sheltered by cottonwoods. Only one window glowed with lamplight through the trees.

He dismounted, staggered, picked up a handful of gravel and tossed it at a front window.

After a minute, the front door opened and Allie Kerrington stepped out onto the veranda. "Who's there?" she challenged. She gripped a rifle and peered into the shadows before recognizing him.

"Lassiter," she cried and ran down the steps. Then a look of concern crossed her smooth features as she came closer to him. "You look even worse than you did in town. I thought you weren't going to accept my invitation. . . ."

Taking his arm, she led him toward the porch steps. Her foreman sang out from the shadowed trees.

"You all right, Miss Kerrington?"

"I'm fine, Davey. Good night." She sighed and started to help Lassiter up the numerous steps. "What you need first is a bath to wash the blood off. And laudanum to kill the pain." She was holding his right hand. "This poor thing. You've been beating anvils with it."

"Quayle's jaw. The same thing."

"He beat you half to death," she said with a quaver in her voice.

"I gave him some of the same." Lassiter's head drooped and he suddenly sank to the porch steps.

"Davey," she called. "I will need you after all. Help me get him to Uncle Mike's room."

The foreman, who had been on his way back to the bunkhouse, came at a run.

11

LASSITER WAS DREAMING ABOUT Owney Devlin and the day he had complained about Charlie Tolliver, the former owner of their ranch.

"Charlie said he'd do some work on the house. It don't look like he's done much."

Then Joe Rudd's voice cut in. "Tolliver got himself killed."

"Charlie Tolliver . . . dead?"

"He was caught with two tied-down calves and a running iron in a fire. He was stealing from one of the members of the pool."

"Which means the pool killed him."

"We look after our own," was Rudd's reply.

Then the scene was washed from Lassiter's mind and he settled into deeper sleep.

Some movement awakened him abruptly. He pried his eyes open and saw a shaft of sunlight streaming through a window. A window where? He rolled his eyes and saw above him the rough planks of a heavy beam ceiling. He tentatively spread his feet and his right one came up against something warm. Something human. He pulled his gaze to the right and saw a mass of auburn hair, relaxed lips, and two green-eyed slits watching him. The lips broke into a warm smile. Suddenly he knew where he was.

"You talk in your sleep," Allie said.

"I do?"

"All about Rudd and Devlin and Charlie Tolliver."

"I was dreaming."

Her hand found his, tightening around the fingers. "What a wonderful night," she whispered.

"Something to remember," he agreed, although his memory as to details was fuzzy.

"I sent one of the men for the doctor."

"For me? I don't need a doctor."

"I'm worried about your ribs."

He placed a hand on his right side and felt soreness. Pressing lightly, he experienced pain. "Yeah," he agreed, "maybe you're right."

"You should have a week of rest."

That brought him upright in bed so suddenly that he winced. His black hair was tousled, his face swollen and bearing abrasions. One eye was swollen and slightly purple. "Can't rest. There's too much to do at DL."

"We won't talk about it now. I'll go cook you some breakfast. I imagine you're starved."

"I could eat a mule," he admitted.

Wearing a wide grin, she hopped out of bed, her slim white body gleaming in the early light. Unself-consciously, she picked up a robe from the back of a chair, fluffed out her long hair at the collar, then covered her nakedness.

The big house seemed unusually quiet, except for a creaking as a strong sun warmed planks that had been chilled by night. He put on his clothes, which were torn and soiled from his battle with Denver Quayle. Every square inch of him seemed bruised or aching. Finally he stamped into his boots and wandered a maze of hallways over Indian rugs with bright patterns until drawn to the kitchen by an aroma of frying bacon. Eggs were sizzling in a pan. Allie poured him a cup of coffee as he sank into a chair at the large kitchen table.

"Here's where Uncle Mike and I took our meals," she said over her shoulder from the big stove. "I haven't used the dining room in ages. . . ." Her voice trailed into a deep sigh. "Too bad you're a ranch owner."

"Why?" he asked, looking up from his steaming cup.

"So you could be my foreman." She sounded wistful. "I'd like to show everyone that I have someone strong on my side at last."

Lassiter said nothing as she set before him a platter of eggs and bacon and fried potatoes, with smaller portions for herself. She watched the big, ravaged man as he ate. A man who had drifted miraculously into her life.

Voices came from the direction of the bunkhouse; the hands were riding out on their daily chores. He could see them through the kitchen window at the fringe of black cottonwoods by the road, slouched in the saddle, wearing wool and faded canvas.

"I wish you were bossing them, Lassiter," she said. "But I know it's impossible."

Cradling a cup of coffee in his two hands, the right one swollen twice its size, he explained that all his energy would have to be directed toward settling the dirty business out at DL. So that Devlin, when he came to his senses, would at least have a half interest in the ranch.

"As of now, he's got nothing. He gave it all to that goddamned Eddie Pyne." Lassiter took a long sip at the coffee cup, set it down and said, "You can see how it is, Allie."

"I almost wish you hadn't come here, seeking sanctuary in the night and me opening my arms to you. . . ."

"I didn't seek sanctuary. I just had a sudden urge to see you."

"Nothing more than two ships passing in the night?"

"More than that and you know it."

She made a vague gesture. "I guess I'm just out of sorts this morning. Of course I'm glad you came to me last night." She reached over and gave his left hand a squeeze.

He helped with the dishes, standing slightly hunched because of the pain in his ribs. She told him to sit down, sounding cross, but he shook his head and stayed on his feet.

"Aside from Devlin there's another thing I've got to settle," he told her.

"What other thing?" She was fishing out a bar of yellow lye soap from the dishpan.

"A man tried for me last night. I killed him." He described the assailant.

When he had finished, she put a hand involuntarily to her throat. "You're sure he was young and bald?"

Lassiter nodded.

"Then it had to be Bishop," she said in a stricken voice. "I'm sure he didn't have brains enough to do anything like that on his own. Someone paid him." She shook her head. "But why . . .?"

"It's the second time he's made a try."

"I remember well the day you killed Bishop's friend, Tex Stillway. Do you think Rudd's behind it?"

"A hunch says maybe. But I dunno for sure. Might be it's just somebody who doesn't like us moving onto the old Tolliver ranch."

"Bishop might've killed you." She whirled and came into his arms, her wet hands cupping his face. "Why do such things have to happen? You should have told me sooner."

He gave a wry grin. "I had other things on my mind."

This caused her to blush slightly but her eyes held his. "Take some of my men and go looking for this skulker who's trying to get you killed."

"I'll do it alone."

"My God, but you're stubborn."

They were still arguing in a rather lighthearted way when Doctor Ambrose Hamilton arrived. A short, plump man wearing wire-framed eyeglasses, he inspected Lassiter. Then he applied arnica to places Allie had missed last night. He probed his ribs, shaking his head. "You be mighty careful for a while," he advised, "until those heal."

He bound them up, making the ties severely tight.

He offered laudanum to ease the pain, but Lassiter refused. He wanted a clear head, not one muddled by a derivative of opium.

Although Allie offered to put the doctor's visit on the ranch bill, Lassiter paid for it himself. Accepting the five-dollar gold piece, the doctor again warned Lassiter about the ribs.

"You take it easy for a few days, then see me in town. But I must say, your opponent is in much worse shape."

"That's comforting news," Allie said with a wink at Lassiter.

"I saw the fight," Doc Hamilton said. "Several times I thought you were a goner. How you ever survived will be marked as one of the miracles of the age."

"No man living can stand up to Lassiter," Allie put in, a touch of pride in her voice.

"That's stretching my luck too far," Lassiter said. "There are plenty of tough men in this world. And luck it was when I faced Quayle."

"You were in superior condition, for one thing," Doc Hamilton said. "Quayle has been abusing his body and after a time the strain of battle began to tell on him."

"I haven't exactly been living in a glass case," Lassiter said with a laugh that brought a twinge of pain.

Lassiter spent a day in bed and then grew restless. When he told Allie he had to leave, she was resigned. "I'm hoping you'll come back after you get things straightened up out at DL. And find out who's hiring people to try and murder you." She shuddered at the word.

He bent his head and kissed lips salty from tears.

"Damn you, Lassiter," she whispered in his arms. "I don't do what we did last night with just anybody."

"I'm sure you don't." Cupping her chin, he smiled down into her attractive face, streaked with tears.

She caught his swollen right hand and held it against her breasts. "For God's sake, don't you go and try to stand up to anybody with a gun. Not with that bad hand."

He nodded. "I'll remember."

One concession he did allow; she had his horse saddled for him. It saved pressure on his ribs. When he mounted up stiffly and turned to look down at her, it was hard to realize they had shared so much in two nights.

With a wave of the hand, he rode off in the direction of DL ranch.

That morning Sid Salone learned that Hi Bishop had been found shot to death on the Apperson road.

He passed the news to Joe Rudd who thoughtfully stroked his jaw. He had just shaved and gave off an aroma of bay rum. His fleshy cheeks were lightly dusted with talcum. "And Bishop was gunning for Lassiter." He peered down at his diminutive foreman with the cold eyes. "Lassiter must've got him."

"Looks that way."

"Maybe I could stir something up with McBride," Rudd mused, thinking of the corpulent sheriff.

"Everybody knows Bishop was a hired gun."

"On the other hand, it might open up a can of worms."

"I still say, give me a chance at Lassiter. Make the price right an' I'll nail him."

Rudd smiled. "I'm sure you could, Sid." Although he had reservations about his foreman putting a gunman such as Lassiter in a grave, there was no denying that Lassiter had been lucky in gunning down Stillway when he and Bishop had tried to box him. And then two nights ago apparently downing Bishop. Maybe Lassiter had been wounded in the fray, he thought hopefully. Or maybe dead.

He thought about DL Ranch. Devlin, in turning his half of it over to his nephew with a quit-claim deed, had left a door ajar. If Rudd could get his foot in it, he could end up owning not only the ranch but the herd of cattle brought from New Mexico.

It would mean just one more nail in the K-27 coffin. Allie Kerrington would be completely surrounded by the Hayfork pool. At which time she might come crawling to beg his forgiveness for rejecting his offer of marriage. Whether he would marry her or not depended on his mood at the time. He spent several leisurely minutes building daydreams in his head at the end of which he wore a broad smile. "The bitch," he said aloud.

Then he fell to thinking about Mrs. Eddie Pyne. Quite a blond morsel. Now if she were suddenly to find herself widowed . . .

He found Salone and reminded him of a visit they had made to DL recently. "Pyne said something about having to leave Missouri in a big hurry. But I didn't pay much attention to it at the time. Do you remember anything about it?"

Salone shook his head.

"Let's take a ride. An' you pick out four good men we can leave at DL."

"What about Lassiter?"

"I'm counting on Lassiter being out of it." He added, "Tell the boys to bring their bedrolls so they can move in."

12

TWO HOURS LATER, RUDD was conferring with Eddie Pyne in the oversized kitchen of the ranch house built of large adz-hewn logs. Eloise had put up curtains which made the place reasonably cheerful. Today she wore a housedress that fit her snugly in the bodice. Rudd watched her ankles as she moved quickly about the kitchen, skirts swirling. She set out three cups on the table where they sat and filled them from a dented enamel pot.

Rudd, smiling, said, "Take your coffee elsewhere, Mrs. Pyne, if you don't mind. What I have to say to your husband is man talk."

She flushed and Eddie looked upset. "Wait a minute—"

"If I'm to help you, Eddie," Rudd interrupted, "you'd better do things my way."

Eddie Pyne thought about it and gave Eloise an imploring look. "Do you mind, honey? We got things to talk about."

"If you invite me, I'll take the noon meal with you

folks," Rudd said pleasantly, but Eloise had left the kitchen, closing the door behind her. She had not taken her cup of coffee.

"What's so important to talk about that she ain't s'posed to hear?" Eddie asked, some of the customary surliness creeping back into his voice.

He told Eddie about the four men he had brought along. "To replace the ones I figure you oughta fire."

"You figurin' to tell me how to run DL?"

"I'm showing you the way, Eddie," Rudd said patiently.

"I dunno about firin' the men."

"Look at it this way, Eddie. The other men are beholden to your uncle. They'll be loyal to him, not you, even though he isn't around."

Eddie blew out his breath. "I s'pose so." Then he added sharply, "But what'll Lassiter say?"

"Not much he can say if the deed's done before he gets back."

"Where you reckon he is, anyhow?"

"Holed up someplace. Nursing his wounds. Might even have a bullet in him." He told Eddie about Hi Bishop's body being found. "There was a lot of blood around, so I hear. Looks like Lassiter might've got shot."

"Why'd he an' that fella Bishop tangle?"

"A grudge is the way I heard it. We can hope that at least Lassiter's laid up for a spell so you and I can get this ranch on a paying basis."

"I'm doin' all right as it is."

"And another thing, we want you in the pool with us."

"That's somethin' I better talk over with Eloise."

"Be sensible, Eddie. A female has no place in men's affairs. You learn that quick or you'll have more'n your share of headaches in life."

A splash of sunlight bathed one wall of the kitchen. The plank floor was still damp from the mopping Eloise had given it earlier. Everywhere was evidence of the work Owney Devlin had put into the place—fresh paint, repaired windows and doors.

Rudd was saying, "We in the pool would rather not have men around who are more loyal to your uncle and Lassiter than they are to us. See what I mean, Eddie?"

"Yeah. How about Tom Hefter? He stays, don't he?"

"He's too old, Eddie. I didn't even bring a man to replace him."

"He . . . he does the cookin'. Eloise, she ain't too good at it."

"Time she learned. You know, I had an understanding with Charlie Tolliver about this place."

"That so?"

"When he got ready to sell out, he was to give me first chance. He didn't."

"My uncle bought it instead. I almost wish I'd never seen the damn place." Eddie's voice shook.

"Tolliver was a smart old bastard. Told me he took out an ad in a Santa Fe paper an' your uncle saw it. 'Course I got to admit that your uncle paid Tolliver more for the place than I'd have done. But still . . . Tolliver give me his word."

"I . . . I can understand." Eddie Pyne didn't like the cold way Rudd was looking at him.

"People who double-cross me don't end up so good."

"What . . . what happened to Tolliver?"

Rudd told him about the two tied-down calves and the running iron being heated in a branding fire. "He won't rustle anybody else's beef, that's for sure."

Eddie's mouth was suddenly dry because he had a feeling there was more to Tolliver's death than the version Rudd had just told him.

"You play the game my way and we'll get along, Eddie." Rudd settled back in his chair, long legs outstretched. "Something I'm curious about, Eddie. That female who was riding with you boys. The one Lassiter stuck up for when I called her a camp woman."

"You mean Ruthie. Yeah, Lassiter did treat her like she was somethin' special." Eddie's mouth twisted. "Reckon he kept her for himself an' after the moon went down, snuck under her blankets."

"How'd she happen to be with you, anyhow?"

Eddie told him about the wrecked wagon and the dead man.

Rudd's brows lifted and he rubbed his chin thoughtfully. "You reckon you could find that grave again?"

"Could find it in my sleep."

"We just might take a look at it one of these days."

"Why?" Eddie wanted to know.

"Just an idea I got in my head," Rudd said with a tight smile. Then he was serious. "Want me with you when you give your men the word? Or are you big enough to do it alone?"

Eddie flushed. "I . . . I can do it."

"I'll wait here for you."

As soon as Eddie Pyne had left by the kitchen door, Rudd hunted up Mrs. Pyne and brought her to the kitchen and sat her down at the table. The feel of her hand, small and warm in his, caused him to experience a sudden erotic surge. He glanced at her breasts outlined under the drab housedress. And he marveled at the size of her waist; he could span it with his two hands, he believed. A delicious morsel, this Mrs. Eloise Pyne.

She stubbornly listened to him explain that running a ranch was a husband's business, not a wife's. He was interrupted by a sudden angry muttering from the yard.

Excusing himself, he picked up his hat and went out. Eddie was faced by his four men and Tom Hefter.

"They want their pay now," a distraught Eddie said, turning to Rudd. "An' I ain't got it."

"Tell 'em to hang around town till the first of the month," Rudd said easily, ignoring them. "By then I'll have bought a few head of cattle off you, Eddie, and you'll have money to pay up."

"He's so anxious to get rid of us," Tom Hefter said, face flushed around the edges of his graying beard, "why don't you give him the money now?"

Rudd eyed the old man. "You'll wait till the first of the month or you won't collect one dime."

"Wait'll Lassiter hears about this," Fred Upshaw said, chewing an end of his thick mustache. Rudd laughed.

"My hunch is strong that Lassiter's out of it," Rudd said, which caused the men to exchange glances.

"You fellas go in the bunkhouse and get packed up," Rudd instructed. And when they protested, Sid Salone added his voice.

"You heard what Mr. Rudd said." Salone's voice

whipped across the yard. Hefter and the four men turned to look at the small Hayfork foreman who had his teeth bared as if daring one of them to reach for a gun. From his stance and the glitter in the eyes, one could draw but one conclusion. He was a gunman, a killer.

When the men had drifted into the bunkhouse, Rudd drew Eddie Pyne aside. "The other day you mentioned leaving Missouri in a helluva big hurry. What was the reason, Eddie?"

Eddie Pyne suddenly looked frightened and glanced over his shoulder as if expecting someone to pounce on him. "It was nothin'," he grunted, his eyes on the ground.

"Tell me, Eddie."

"Don't want to talk about it."

"How many friends you got here, Eddie?"

Eddie licked his lips and thought about it. "None, I reckon. Not even my uncle now."

"If somebody from Missouri came nosing around, you might need a friend—meaning me. Get it off your chest. Tell me about Missouri."

Haltingly, Eddie told him about his aunt dying and how after the funeral he had asked a girl to go with him to a school dance. She had already been asked by Clyde Kaney, but said she'd rather go with Eddie. One thing led to another. Guns were drawn. It turned out to be Eddie's lucky day. Kaney lay dying at his feet, screaming, "My brother'll kill you for what you done to me!"

A terrified Eddie Pyne grabbed what money his late aunt had hidden around the house and headed for New Mexico and his Uncle Owney Devlin.

"The Kaneys don't know where I am," Eddie said, his voice strained from recounting the events of the tragic day. "I hope they never find out." He took a deep breath. "Right off, one thing me an' Eloise had in common was that we had both lived in Missouri. But her in St. Louis an' me in a place no bigger'n a good-sized pimple."

Rudd took the noon meal with Eddie and Eloise; the men were still in the bunkhouse. The meal was something warmed up that Tom Hefter had cooked the evening before. She scorched the beans and the beef was dried out from being overcooked in the frying pan.

"I'll send over a man who can cook," Rudd said, crumbling a cold biscuit in thick gravy, "until you get the hang of it yourself."

Eloise glared across the table. "Mr. Rudd, I do wish you'd stay out of our business."

Eddie whitened but Rudd took it with a shrug and a faint smile. "I know how you feel, Mrs. Pyne, but out here you'll find things are done differently than back where you came from."

Sounds of an approaching horse caused them to look around. Through a kitchen window they saw Lassiter.

Eddie Pyne swore under his breath. "He's alive after all."

13

LASSITER, HIS HAT PULLED low to shadow his ravaged features, took only a moment to assess the situation. He saw his men carrying out their warbags from the bunkhouse, four men with bedrolls waiting to enter. The latter group eyed him warily and looked around for Sid Salone, who came strutting up with his cocky rooster walk, to plant himself in front of Lassiter.

"Figured maybe you went back to New Mexico," said the little man thinly.

"I like it here in Arizona," Lassiter drawled. His men were frozen by the bunkhouse door. He singled out Upshaw. "What's going on?"

Upshaw spoke bitterly, "We've been fired."

"Well, you're unfired. Put your stuff back."

"Wait a minute," Salone cut in. "Rudd's tryin' to do Eddie Pyne a favor."

"He forgot one small item. I own half of this ranch." Lassiter stood tall, both hands shoved deep in the pockets of his Levis.

Salone studied the bulge made by Lassiter's hands

in his pockets, then flicked his small dark eyes to the .44 belted at the waist. He gave Lassiter a speculative look.

In those moments with the sun directly overhead, a faint breeze stirring the trees, tension in the yard was a silent scream.

"Don't try anything, Salone," Lassiter warned coldly, his eyes locked to the small dark face.

Presently, beads of sweat appeared on Salone's forehead and he looked away. It seemed to anger him that Lassiter had stared him down. He wheeled and stalked over to where Joe Rudd was just stepping out the kitchen door. The urbane Rudd, gold links of his watch chain sparkling in the sunlight, touched a handkerchief to his lips, then stuffed it in a pocket.

"Well, well, Lassiter," he boomed with a smile. "We'd about given you up."

"Never do that."

"You do seem to have an uncommon run of good luck."

"My luck comes and goes like everybody else's."

"I'm thinking particularly of Denver Quayle. And Hi Bishop. His body was found."

Lassiter's cold smile stretched across his white teeth. "Rudd, I'll have to ask you to get your men the hell off this ranch."

Rudd's eyes darkened. "I was only trying to do Eddie Pyne a favor. . . ."

"That's what your foreman tried to tell me."

Eddie Pyne stood as if frozen on a step below the kitchen doorway, his white-faced wife peering anxiously over his shoulder.

As had Salone, Rudd also seemed to find the bulge

of Lassiter's hands in his pockets of interest—especially the right hand. He lifted his head, his eyes bright. "The fight with Quayle crippled you up, I reckon."

"No."

"Let's have a look at your hands then." Rudd smiled triumphantly and Sid Salone, standing nearby, came up on the toes of his small boots.

Eloise sensed the buildup of tension and screamed, "No! I won't have it! There's already been enough violence in our lives!"

"Go back inside, Mrs. Pyne," Lassiter said without turning his head. "So you won't get hurt. In case Rudd or some other fool tries to push me."

Rudd bit his lips and backed up a step, as if weighing the gamble whether Lassiter's right hand was sound or crippled. Tom Hefter decided the matter by appearing in the barn door with a shotgun leveled.

"The boss told you to git out!" the old man said evenly. "So *git!*"

"There's more'n one boss here," Rudd said, his voice beginning to shred with anger. "Eddie Pyne happens to own a half interest—"

"Seems like you're the one forgetting that, Rudd," Lassiter pointed out coldly. "The way you come over here giving orders."

"Please!" Eloise cried. "Don't let this ugliness continue."

"As you wish, Mrs. Pyne," Rudd responded, seeing a way out to save his face. He mounted up and gave Eloise a jaunty wave of the hand. The men he had brought with him had packed up their bedrolls and were now following Rudd out of the yard.

Only when they were gone did Tom Hefter lower the shotgun. "Lassiter, you look a sight," the old man remarked, coming from the barn. "What happened to you?"

"I tried to waltz with a grizzly bear."

Lassiter went to the bunkhouse and flung himself onto the bench. Hefter and the four men followed him and stared in shock at sight of Lassiter's right hand now resting on the table.

"Jeezus Keeryst," Hefter exclaimed after a moment of assessing the swollen hand. "You could no more pull a gun with that hand than I could fry bacon on a sheet of newspaper. An' you bluffed 'em, you did." The old man grinned widely and unloaded the shotgun. "But you better lie low till that hand heals up."

"I figure to," Lassiter said tersely.

He asked details about Rudd's attempt to replace them with his own men. When Hefter and the others had offered their versions, Lassiter swore under his breath.

"The nerve of that bastard. But that's one thing he was always long on . . . nerve."

Later that day Eddie Pyne also got a close look at Lassiter's right hand. He swallowed and was tempted to draw his gun. In fact, he even let a hand drop to the butt of his belted gun. But then he found Lassiter's eyes on him. He instantly released it as if it was hot. Sweat popped out at his hairline and he hurried into the house.

With two of his men, Lassiter followed the tracks of Rudd and company for a few miles to make sure they weren't hanging around and planning more mischief.

As Lassiter was unsaddling back at the ranch,

Eloise came across the yard, her pale hair blowing in the breeze. If he hadn't known what a conniving bitch she really was, he might have been put off by the look of sweetness about her now.

"I sense you don't like us very much, Mr. Lassiter," she said, coming right to the point. "But as long as we're going to share this ranch, I think we should all make an attempt to get along—to stuff our feelings into a bag and buckle the straps. It's what my father used to say."

She had spoken bluntly and so did he. "It isn't that I don't like you. I just can't forget that you two went behind Owney Devlin's back."

She twisted her hands together. "We should have faced up to him, I admit."

"So you've said."

"But Eddie had a little money and all we could think about was getting away as far and as fast as possible."

"Well, you'd have made it. If Devlin hadn't been so crazy to get himself married that he chased after you."

"Lassiter, I had hoped to make amends so that we could understand each other better." Her lower lip trembled. "As long as we're to be partners . . ."

"Partners," he snorted. "Yeah, it seems that we are."

"I intend to make the best of this dreadful situation."

With that, she turned on her heel and walked away.

Lassiter took the rest of the week to recover from his bout with Quayle. On Sunday, his right hand was nearly back to normal. So he went a mile or so from the ranch house and practiced shooting at some trees.

Join the Western Book Club
and GET 4 FREE* BOOKS NOW!
A $19.96 VALUE!

Yes! I want to subscribe to the Western Book Club.

Please send me my **4 FREE* BOOKS**. I have enclosed $2.00 for shipping/handling. Each month I'll receive the four newest Leisure Western selections to preview for 10 days. If I decide to keep them, I will pay the Special Members Only discounted price of just $3.36 each, a total of $13.44, plus $2.00 shipping/handling ($19.50 US in Canada). This is a **SAVINGS OF AT LEAST $6.00** off the bookstore price. There is no minimum number of books I must buy, and I may cancel the program at any time. In any case, the **4 FREE* BOOKS** are mine to keep.

*In Canada, add $5.00 shipping/handling per order for the first shipment. For all future shipments to Canada, the cost of membership is $16.25 US, which includes shipping and handling. (All payments must be made in US dollars.)

NAME: _____

ADDRESS: _____

CITY: _____ **STATE:** _____

COUNTRY: _____ **ZIP:** _____

TELEPHONE: _____

E-MAIL: _____

SIGNATURE: _____

He was fairly well satisfied with the results. Confident that he was once again a whole man after the severe beating he had suffered from the savage Denver Quayle, Lassiter rode out to Apperson's to see if there was any news of Owney Devlin.

He found him living in a shack about two hundred yards east of the place. It was in a box canyon surrounded on three sides by towering walls of red rock. Purple waves of sage danced in the sunlight. Ruthie had brought rugs from Apperson's and fixed the place up as best she could.

"Anybody home?" Lassiter called.

Ruthie, sounding sleepy, spoke from the shadowed interior of the dismal place. "Wait'll I put something on."

Lassiter smiled to himself at the irony of her modesty. She came out front, blinking at the strong sunlight, and apologized for having still been in bed.

"I worked real late last night," she explained.

Lassiter peered back into the house. "Owney all right?"

"He's still asleep. I tried to wake him up when I got home, but he was too far gone. Still is."

"The jug?"

She nodded. There were dark circles under her eyes. "He drinks most of the time."

"I've come to take him home."

"He won't go. I'm sure of that."

"I think I can manage."

She gave him a long look out of her shadowed eyes. "He'll pull a gun on you if you try. He's told me that much."

Lassiter patted her arm. "You leave it to me,

Ruthie.'' He cleared his throat. "Listen, I've got a few dollars put away. The Prescott stage is due tomorrow. Once you're there, you can figure out where you want to go, what you want to do."

"Owney's the first person in my life I've ever been able to take care of. I'm not giving him up."

"Not much of a life for you . . . or for him."

"I live from minute to minute, Lassiter. And so does he."

"He's living off what you earn at Apperson's."

"You make it sound ugly."

"It is. I thought you told me you wanted to start a new life after your friend Pete got himself killed in the wagon. And here you are, right back into it again."

"Out here in the West there's only three kinds of women. Dried-up old maids, the married kind, or . . . my kind."

"You could work in a store. Go back to Wayfield . . ."

"They'd laugh me out of town. Or run me out. Or maybe be generous and give me a crib in the *congal.*"

"You could at least *try!*"

"Owney needs me and I live for him. For no other reason, Lassiter. None at all. If you'll excuse me, I've got to get dressed. Apperson wants me in early today."

She went back inside. Their voices had awakened Devlin. Lassiter found him propped up on an elbow, sucking on a glass of whiskey. He looked ten years older, his face thin and lined, nearly covered by a full beard. Small veins crisscrossed his nose and his eyes were sunset red.

"'Lo, Lassiter," he grunted. "I heard you two talkin' about me."

Lassiter pulled up a chair beside the rumpled bed and sat down. Ruthie leaned over and kissed Devlin on the cheek, lifted a hand to Lassiter, then started the walk to Apperson's.

Lassiter was glad to be alone with Devlin. Carefully he explained that Devlin's rightful place was back at DL and to hell with the quit-claim deed.

When he had finished, Devlin shook his head. "I've made my bed an' I'm layin' in it."

Lassiter argued, pleaded, but Devlin was adamant. Lassiter's temper began to thin. "One day when we first started out from New Mexico, Tom Hefter told me he hoped to hell you never took another drink as long as you lived. I can see what he meant."

Devlin's mouth twisted. "I likely never would've taken another drink after my dear sister Rose got killed, but . . ." Tears sparkled in Devlin's eyes. "Damn it, Lassiter, Eddie's her son. Me findin' him in bed with the gal I figured to marry was like gettin' hit over the head with a sledgehammer."

"Other men have had surprises and not come apart at the seams!"

"It's me bein' paid back for the day I was layin' there passed-out drunk an' not stoppin' Rose from ridin' off with her no-good husband drivin' a half-broke team." Devlin put a hand over his eyes. His other hand was buried under the blankets.

He sat up after a minute, his thick, hairy legs swung over the edge of the bed. Sobs shook his big frame as Lassiter watched. Finally, Devlin got himself under control.

"It's the Lord payin' me back for lettin' my dear sweet little sister get herself killed. . . ." He gave a violent shake of his head as if to cut off further memories of the tragic day. Tears arced down his cheek as sunlight streamed through the upper half of a side window. Boards had been nailed across the lower half where the glass was missing. The place smelled of dust and stale grease.

"Get your clothes on, Owney. I'm taking you home."

"It's Eddie's place now, yours an' Eddie's."

"You gave it to him when you were upset. Take it back."

"*I want him to have it!*" Devlin's bloodshot eyes glared. "Can't you git that through your head?"

Lassiter reached out for him, but Devlin withdrew his right hand from under the blankets. It gripped a cocked .45.

"Don't make me shoot, Lassiter." He was having a hard time retaining control.

Lassiter debated. In Devlin's condition, he could be tricked. Then what? Knock him cold? Take him back to DL trussed up like a hog to market?

"Think about this, Owney. You know what they say about men who live off women like Ruthie."

"Get out of here, Lassiter. Don't come back!"

From the doorway, Lassiter glanced into the house and saw that Devlin was filling his glass from a bottle.

On his way home, Lassiter stopped off at Apperson's and tried to get Ruthie to listen to him. But she was determined to stay with Devlin. It seemed she had needed someone to care for all of her short life and had found it in the big man who was well on the road to drinking himself to death. This fact he pointed out to Ruthie, but she just gave him a worried look and shook her head.

She did offer one concession. "I'll try and see that Owney doesn't drink so much."

"I like you, Ruthie, like you a lot. But you're so goddamn stubborn."

"I suppose."

"Seems like most of you young females are these days." He was thinking of Allie Kerrington, who had stubbornly refused to accept the fact that he didn't want to become her foreman. He thought of Eloise Pyne, stubbornly determined to make the most of a bad situation. And Ruthie, clinging to a hopeless drunk.

14

"SOMETHING TO THINK ABOUT, Vince—that Bishop killing." Rudd was in town, talking to the sheriff.

"Yeah, there's been a lot of talk about that," McBride admitted. "First off there was Tex Stillway . . ."

"We know for sure Lassiter killed him."

"So Allie Kerrington said. But in self-defense."

"He sure as hell waylaid Hi Bishop. It's what I came to tell you. You claim folks are beginning to talk about the killings. Well, there's one you can solve pronto."

McBride slouched in a swivel chair in his small office, his feet on a cluttered rolltop desk. "And there was that Charlie Tolliver killin'." McBride slanted his gaze at Rudd who straddled a straight-backed chair. Rudd's expression didn't change.

"That's another matter, Vince," Rudd said bluntly. "You know damn well it is. What I'm interested in now—and you should be—is Hi Bishop's death."

"Was he a special friend of yours, Joe?"

"Hell, no," Rudd said a little too quickly so that a spare smile broke above McBride's double chin. "You can sew Lassiter up for his murder."

"Were you there when it happened?"

"No."

"Then how do you know Lassiter done it?"

"Hunch."

"A hunch ain't worth a damn in Judge Quincy's court. An' that ol' bastard is due here purty soon. Wrote me a letter sayin' he ain't satisfied with how my office is run here. Says the killin' has got to stop."

"Bring Lassiter up before Judge Quincy—"

"Hold it right there, Joe. I gotta have evidence to do that. An' there ain't a damn speck of it." McBride leveled a fat forefinger at Rudd. "An' you watch out with that pool of yours, Joe. At least don't stir things up till after the judge leaves town. Thank God the ol' bastard won't be here but one day."

Sobered by the sheriff's warning, Rudd stopped by DL on the way home. He decided it was time to gamble. Lassiter was alone in the bunkhouse, trying to make sense of Devlin's rather slipshod bookkeeping. There didn't seem to be anyone else around. The first thing Rudd noticed upon entering the bunkhouse was Lassiter's gun rig hanging on a peg on a bunk behind his head.

Lassiter scowled as Rudd waved his hands to show that his visit was peaceful. He threw a leg over the bench opposite Lassiter and sat down.

"What do you want, Rudd?" Lassiter demanded coolly.

"I'm here to make you a reasonable offer for your half of this place."

"I'm not selling." Lassiter's eyes were hard, but the affable Rudd was not to be swayed.

"You've got a rep for not staying too long in one place, Lassiter. This is your chance to see new territory. The land here's not worth much but I'll give you market price for your share of the beef. Five hundred head or thereabouts."

"And when I'm riding out with my pockets full of money, some gents stick guns in my face and take it?"

It was so close to the truth that Rudd was barely able to keep surprise from showing. "You're damned suspicious of a man," he said, managing a smile.

"Of you, 'specially."

A corner of Rudd's mouth twitched. "I rode over here to make you a decent offer for your share of this place. . . ." He drew a deep breath, then said, "All right, I'll give you five dollars an acre for your share of the land. How's that?"

"I'll tell you why I won't sell. Because Owney Devlin is coming back on this ranch as my partner."

"Pretty hard to do after he deeded his half over to Eddie Pyne."

"That can be handled."

"Kick Eddie and his bride off the place?"

Lassiter looked him in the eye. "Like I said, it can be handled."

Rudd climbed to his feet and stood looking down at Lassiter at the table. He inclined his head at Lassiter's right hand that rested on a worn ledger. "Your hand looks good as new."

"Yeah."

"Quite a bluff you played on us the other day."

"You'll never know for sure, Rudd."

"I can guess." Rudd's smile was tight. "Maybe we should've taken a chance and settled things once and for all. Just maybe."

Lassiter's smile was equally hard. "Tom with the shotgun is what settled the mud in the puddle."

"Well, I just made a friendly visit. But seems you won't have it that way."

"All I did was tell you how things stood. That one way or another, Devlin is coming back here."

Rudd glanced again at Lassiter's gun rig hanging from a peg on one of the bunks. Then he started for the door of the bunkhouse. Suddenly, he spun around, his right hand slapping toward his holstered revolver. But he came up short when he saw that in that handful of seconds Lassiter had reached back, drawn his .44 and cocked it.

Rudd's face reddened but he lowered his hand and managed to speak in a reasonably level voice. "Think over my offer. It's a good one."

Then he stalked out, with Lassiter's laughter ringing in his ears.

A day later Lassiter was moving cattle when he ran into Allie Kerrington and two of her men. Les Boyle had short legs and a long torso, which gave him an overbalanced appearance. He gave Lassiter a nod. The other man, Si Bellarmine, was chunky and in his forties. He looked Lassiter over.

Allie wore a boy's shirt and faded Levis. Today there was tension at the corners of her pretty mouth but she pretended cheerfulness. They stood apart from the others in the shade of a post oak, their horses munching grass.

They made small talk until she got around to what was on her mind—Lassiter coming in with her. "Have you thought about it?" she asked, watching his face.

He lifted his shoulder and let it settle. "Some," he admitted. "But I can't make a move till I get Devlin back on DL."

"Just how will you manage that?"

"Seems I'm between a rock and a hard place where it comes to Owney Devlin."

"I can't stop thinking about our nights together."

"Runs through my mind, too." He reached out to gently stroke her arm. A small shiver went through her body at his touch.

"Why do things have to be so . . . so complicated?" she asked in despair. "Devlin's a grown man; can't he look after himself?"

"I sometimes wonder just how grown up he is."

"Besides, how in the world would you ever talk his nephew into giving back his half interest in the ranch?"

"I could handle that part of it. But Devlin won't listen. In time he will," he added quickly.

"Eloise appears demure on the surface but under that smooth skin is cold steel. I sensed it in the few times I talked with her."

"Yeah," Lassiter sighed. "She's got her little hands on half a ranch and she's not ready to let go. But I'll make her see the light."

"Oh, Lassiter, I wish . . ." Allie made a despondent gesture.

Lassiter didn't let her finish whatever it was she intended to say. He changed the subject to Joe Rudd. "Has he made any funny moves lately?"

She shook her head. "He's been keeping away from me. Why, I don't know. Before you came, I found it hard to get rid of him."

"You think he suspects us of more than holding hands?"

"I don't care if he does," she said firmly.

Before swinging into the saddle, she gave him her hand and looked up into his dark eyes. "You're the first man in ages who has stirred me." Then she gave a funny little laugh and added, "Don't let the fire go out."

With flushed cheeks, she rode away with her two men. Some distance down the road she turned and waved. He lifted a hand. She was a remarkable young lady, he had to admit, able to stand up for herself in a male world. That took sheer guts, or maybe it was gumption. Somehow that suited her better.

After her visit, his mood lightened and the day went swiftly. But there was still one problem. He was running short of cash. He had a conference with Eddie Pyne. "I think we oughta sell two hundred head of beef."

"Go ahead, sell," the younger man said indifferently. Then his blue eyes sharpened. "But just remember to give me half the money."

Before leaving to dicker with a cattle buyer he knew to be in the area, Eloise asked him to take supper with them. She was making an effort to heal the breach, he had to admit. Tom Hefter had been teaching her the rudiments of ranch cooking and she had prepared tonight's meal on her own. She wore a white dress decorated with small yellow flowers for the occasion, most of it covered by a bulky apron. Tendrils of blond hair were damp from perspiration and her pretty face was flushed from stove heat. Even Eddie was dressed up in his black suit, his hair slicked with pomade.

The roast she cooked was overdone, the potatoes mealy and the gravy had the consistency of flour paste. Eddie turned up his nose but didn't say anything. Eloise picked at her food.

"I'm hoping we can be friends," Eloise finally got around to saying. Most of the time she had been staring at her plate as if to ask herself what had gone wrong with the meal. When she spoke, her voice was reedy at first, then stronger. "It's silly for anyone to have a grudge. Don't you think so, Mr. Lassiter?"

"Reckon," he said, chewing hard on a piece of tough beef.

"I know you think we did wrong . . . and maybe we did. But who's to judge? As long as we're going to own this ranch together, I think we should get along."

Lassiter sighed and blew on a cup of hot coffee—the only good part of the meal. He wondered what she'd say when he finally was able to talk sense into Devlin and end this farce. Ruthie had told him she had kept whiskey away from Devlin as much as possible and what he drank she had watered down first. Devlin was gradually coming around, she had confided on his last visit.

That was good news indeed.

Lassiter left shortly after dawn for his rendezvous with the cattle buyer.

As soon as Lassiter pulled out, Eddie Pyne saddled up and headed for Joe Rudd's Hayfork Ranch.

15

"YOU TOLD ME TO let you know whenever Lassiter figured to be gone for a spell," Eddie reminded Rudd in the latter's ranch yard.

"Yeah, I remember," Rudd admitted. But that was when he'd had other plans. Since then he had decided to hit Lassiter where it hurt, but deviously. He knew the man was fond of Ruthie. And Lassiter's friend, Owney Devlin, was harnessed up with her.

Rudd placed a hand on Eddie's shoulder. "Show me that grave, Eddie, the one with Ruthie's man in it."

Eddie rubbed his jaw and looked pained. "Jeez, I dunno if I can find it."

"You were sure you could find it when we talked about it before," Rudd said coldly.

Something in Rudd's voice drained Eddie Pyne's face. "Yeah . . . I . . . I reckon I can find it."

Sid Salone rode with them, bringing along a pair of short-handled shovels. "You and Sid can do the digging," Rudd said. "I got a bad back."

Salone turned his hard, diminutive face on Rudd but didn't say anything.

It took them most of the afternoon backtracking the slow-moving herd. But finally they came upon the old road and the grave at the bottom of the steep grade. Fortunately, the dirt was still soft and Eddie and Salone had no trouble uncovering the body. It had been wrapped in a tarpaulin from the wagon that still stood on its crushed wheels where it had landed after turning over and spilling the occupants. Ruthie had been thrown clear, but her companion had not fared as well.

Eddie shuddered at the sight of the decomposing body. "Like Lassiter said, a busted neck is what done him in." Eddie's voice shook.

"Busted neck isn't what done him in," Rudd said through the handkerchief he was holding over his mouth and nose. "Bullet hole in the back of the head killed him."

Eddie pinched his nostrils and leaned down. The body had been unrolled from the moldy tarp and now lay in a prone position. Rudd spoke to Sid Salone and the dark little man drew his gun and fired a bullet into the back of the skull. Chips of bone flew into the sunlight.

The sound of the sudden shot made Eddie jump. He didn't know exactly what Rudd was up to but when he felt the man's eyes on him he got a hollow feeling in his stomach.

"Eddie, you're gonna swear you saw that bullet hole when Lassiter was burying him. But you didn't say anything. Then, your conscience got to bothering you and you told me about it. Understand?"

"Yeah, but . . ." Eddie Pyne swallowed under Rudd's unblinking stare. "Yeah, I understand," he said in a weak voice.

"Sid, you stay here and keep an eye on him," pointing at the corpse. "Me and Eddie got business in Wayfield."

It was late afternoon by the time they reached town. Rudd found Sheriff Vince McBride at the Four Aces with a glass in his hand. His broad face was flushed. He was talking to three members of the Hayfork pool: Parkie Dolan, Doc Plane and Jeff Snedecor. They greeted Rudd and looked at Eddie Pyne narrowly.

"Eddie's got a story to tell, Vince," Rudd said to the sheriff. "Go ahead, Eddie."

"In here?"

"These fellas are friends of mine."

Everyone crowded around to listen. When Eddie realized the rapt attention he was getting as he started his tale, he swelled with importance. After an awkward start, the words flowed smoothly and he told it dramatically. Even Cavendish came over from the bar to listen.

"That whore killed her pimp," Rudd said when Eddie had finished. "Shot him in the back of the head."

"What you want me to do about it?" Vince McBride whined.

"Make an example of her. You told me yourself the circuit judge has been on your neck about the killings around here. Show him how you cleared one up, anyhow. When's he due, by the way?"

"Day after tomorrow."

Rudd, with a fierce smile, looked around at the

faces. "Most of you hombres have got wives and kids. You want 'em breathing the same air as that foul female out at Apperson's?"

The men looked at each other and shifted their feet. "Course we don't," said Doc Plane. He was tall and angular with a courtly manner and an Adam's apple as big as a knuckle. He had once been connected with a medicine show.

Plans were quickly made and the services of Walt Berryman, the undertaker, engaged. The following day he was to take a wagon and a coffin over to the unmarked grave, collect a body and bring it back into town.

"We want him in one piece if possible," Rudd explained. "Packing him in by horseback could change that in a hurry, from the condition he's in."

Eddie's lips were dry when he finally got Rudd aside and said, "What about Lassiter in all this? He'll raise holy hell."

"I've got a little plan to keep him occupied until it's over with." He beckoned to Doc Plane who hurried over to their corner of the saloon and listened to Rudd's whispered words.

Then he straightened up, wearing a hard smile. "Will get it done, Joe," and he hurried out.

It was midafternoon of the following day. Ruthie was helping the other girls clean up when Sheriff Vince McBride and several men rode into the yard.

Apperson was fooling around at the piano and his one good eye beamed when he saw McBride. He called out that he was to help himself to whiskey and whatever else he wanted. He smiled and gave the sheriff a broad wink.

"I'm here on business, Apperson," McBride said in his official-sounding voice. When he moved, rolls of fat rippled under his clothing. "Is one of your gals named Ruthie?"

Apperson's good eye turned cold. "Why you want to know?"

"Just wanta talk to her . . . in town."

"That's all he wants to do," Rudd interjected.

Apperson got up from the piano, his eyepatch in shadow. "Has this got somethin' to do with Pete Shamrock, by any chance?"

"So that's his name," Rudd said.

"He was a no-good son of a bitch," Apperson said. "She told me what happened to him."

Rudd and McBride exchanged glances. Rudd gave a faint shake of his head. He didn't want McBride saying too much. Hardcases hung out at Apperson's and there was no sense in stirring up trouble.

Apperson called Ruthie over and introduced her to McBride, who stood looking down his overripe nose at her. "We'll take a ride," he announced and got her by an arm.

"It's all right, Ruthie," Apperson assured her. He had to keep on the good side of Sheriff McBride, no matter what.

A horse was provided for her. She hiked her skirts up and rode with them, her back straight, chin up. But the palms of her hands were clammy and her heart beat too rapidly.

They just wanted her to identify someone, the sheriff had told her.

It was a long ride and nearly dark when they reached Wayfield. She was taken immediately to the undertaker's behind the Wayfield Furniture Store. McBride handed her a clean white handkerchief.

"Better put it over your nose," he advised in a gravelly voice.

The undertaker, a roly-poly, harassed-looking little man, removed the coffin lid. Ruthie almost fainted from the odor.

"You ever seen this fella before?" McBride asked her.

"It's . . . it's Pete," she could tell from what was left of his face. She shuddered.

"Pete Shamrock?"

"It's what he called himself. But I never did think it was his real name."

"Don't matter none." McBride beckoned with a fat forefinger. "Mr. Pyne, will you step forward, please?"

Eddie, who had been lurking in the background, avoided Ruthie's eyes. "Yeah, sheriff?"

"Mr. Pyne, did this female confess to you that she shot this here Pete Shamrock in cold blood?"

"She did."

Ruthie stood dumbfounded.

The sheriff said, "Gents, I'd like you to come close an' look at the bullet hole in the back of this poor fella's skull. In the *back*, remember I said." Adjustments were made to the corpse.

Men crowded forward to look and then put their eyes on Ruthie, who by now was held by McBride in case she might try to run.

Ruthie was locked up in the Wayfield jail.

The circuit judge, having finished his business to the north of Wayfield sooner than expected, appeared in town the following morning. When he heard about the murder case, he hurried through other matters he was supposed to hear: complaints of a sheep rancher, an argument over riparian rights and a boy accused of stealing a mule.

Wayfield had never housed a female prisoner before, so adjustments had to be made. Blankets were strung over bars to give her privacy.

McBride brought her some breakfast from the cafe. She clutched at his arm. "Will you get word to Lassiter?" she begged.

"You eat an' then get some rest."

He backed out of the cell and locked her in, then went to the jail office where several men were gathered, among them Joe Rudd.

"She wanted me to get word to Lassiter," McBride confided in a low voice.

"Anybody but him," Rudd responded. "With luck, he'll be out of it."

16

ALLIE KERRINGTON WAS JUST mounting up that morning when Lassiter rode into her yard. Her look of anxiety and surprise completely washed away his broad smile. She said, "You've heard, then."

He reined in beside her horse. "Heard what? I only rode over to see how you were getting along."

"Poorly, it seems. I was just on my way over to your place."

His lips tightened. "I smell trouble."

She nodded, saying that Doc Plane had dropped by to tell her that he had spotted about one hundred head of K-27 cattle and at least twenty-five from DL being driven by rustlers toward Bull's Head in the mountains. That was yesterday.

Lassiter was instantly suspicious. "Isn't Plane a member of the Hayfork pool?"

"Yes, but he's always been more friendly than the others."

That didn't prove anything to Lassiter. "Is he going with you?"

"The poor man has a bad leg. It pained him to ride this far to alert me. He's gone home." Lassiter's hesitation caused her to frown. "I'm going after them."

"How'd he know they were rustlers?" Lassiter asked skeptically.

"From the way the herd was being pushed—fast. He watched them from a ridge. They weren't from these parts. I swear, I don't know which way to turn. Except to you." Her eyes were imploring. "Davey's no help, he's sick with the grippe. A man his age should be sitting on a porch with his feet on the railing—not out chasing rustlers."

He glanced through the trees toward the silent bunkhouse in the morning shadows. "How about your men?" he asked, not wishing to be drawn into it. But after all, if twenty-five head of DL beef had been driven away . . .

He saw Boyle and Richter come riding up through the black cottonwoods and draw rein. "Where's the rest of the crew?" Lassiter wanted to know.

She drew a deep breath and exhaled sharply. "They haven't been paid." He waved a hand at Richter and Boyle. "They're the only ones who didn't let that stand in the way of helping me out."

He gave them a nod and they all rode to the spot where Doc Plane had spotted the rustlers. It did look as if over a hundred head of cattle had been driven rapidly west, their bunched tracks leaving a fresh scar through the chaparral.

"Allie, you better get home," Lassiter said, studying the trail. "I'll get my men and with Boyle and Richter we'll handle it."

She shook her head. Her hair glistened in the sunlight. "My cattle, my responsibility."

"But you asked me for help and I'm telling you how it oughta be done." He didn't like the risk of her being underfoot and perhaps getting hurt. Memories of their nights together were vivid in his mind.

The more he argued, however, the more adamant she became. At last he gave up and the four of them rode for DL.

When they got there, Lassiter told Eddie Pyne what had happened. But Eddie only muttered something under his breath and went into the house. A slammed door was an indication of his mood. For the past two days, Eddie had been more sullen and noncommunicative than usual. Lassiter rubbed his chin, wondering what was eating the younger man. But he had no time to dwell on it because of what lay ahead. Lassiter rounded up his crew, left Tom Hefter behind to keep an eye on things and rode out with Allie and her two ranch hands.

Although Lassiter felt differently toward Richter and Boyle for remaining loyal to Allie, he still remembered all too well the attempts on his life by two of the K-27 crew, Tex Stillway and Hi Bishop.

Lassiter estimated that the cattle in question had been rustled within the last two days, which meant they couldn't be far. The grade through a long valley steepened. Allie bit her lips when Lassiter eased his rifle in the saddle scabbard. His blue eyes were staring ahead at the trail through a great expanse of purple sage spread out to a distant barrier of red rock in tortured configurations, due to some great upheaval of nature centuries past.

When the sun was directly overhead, they pushed on, not taking time for a midday rest. It was an hour later that Lassiter noticed that the cattle were no longer in a herd but were spread out. And his sharp eyes noted that the tracks of five horses had cut away to the north.

He drew rein, scowling. They were in a forested canyon, bisected by a rambling creek. Their presence caused a great flock of birds to wheel into the air.

"What is it, Lassiter?" Allie asked, turning back to where he sat his saddle. Lassiter pointed and told her the obvious.

She was perplexed. "But why would they drive them this far and just turn them loose?"

"I dunno," Lassiter said grimly. "It just don't make sense." Or did it?

"I wonder if you were taken in by Doc Plane," he speculated.

Her green eyes were thoughtful. "He's always such a . . . gentleman with his courtly manners. And he was a great friend of my father's."

"But that was before Rudd moved onto Diablo range."

"Yes, that's so. But what's the purpose of all this?" She gestured at the cattle tracks.

Perhaps to have them both away so they could be burned out, was the thought that streaked across his mind. But he didn't voice it. He suggested to Allie that she accompany the men driving the cattle back to their own range. He wanted to look around. As usual she argued, but this time he shook his head and firmly said, "No." He intended to go alone.

Tracks of the rustlers were easy to follow. There

were five of them, as near as he could tell. After crossing a series of low hills, the tracks angled back toward the foot of the mountains.

Always alert, he followed the trail down through cottonwoods, past gargoyle shapes of limestone. The shadows were thick, but after a few miles red rock cliffs gave way to forested slopes. Ahead were miles of sage slopes. He followed the flow of an amber creek until ahead he saw a promontory, and on it a faint brownish bulge. Squinting against the sun, he rode closer until able to make out a small building. Beside it was a corral holding two horses.

Lassiter approached warily, pulled into a screen of gnarled junipers and watched the building for perhaps five minutes. A glance at the sun told him it was probably an hour past noon. Ahead he could see where three of the horsemen he had been following had veered sharply to the east, but two had gone to the shack on the shelf of rock.

A man stepped from the shack, emptied a pan of water, then went back inside and closed the door. It was too far to tell who it was.

Leaving his horse, Lassiter moved forward on foot. He started up a zigzag trail that led to the shelf above. He climbed, gun in hand, carefully avoiding all rocks and loose dirt that might start a minor avalanche and alert those in the building. Now he could tell that the building was a line shack for one of the Diablo range ranches. But he wasn't familiar enough with the territory yet to know which one.

But he intended to find out. As Lassiter neared the shack, a breeze that had been blowing strongly suddenly shifted so that the two horses in the corral picked up his scent. They whinnied.

From inside the shack came a booming voice. "Pinky, go take a look around."

"Yeah, Sam."

Lassiter ducked behind a knob of rock screened with greasewood and waited. He saw a wide-shouldered man wearing suspenders. The breeze stirred his bushy beard. Scowling, he crouched and peered around the four points of the compass. Clouds had rolled in, momentarily screening the sun. A coyote began to yap farther up the mountain.

Pinky called into the shack. "That musta been what stirred up the hosses."

He went back inside and closed the door.

From what Lassiter could tell, there were only two of them, which was good.

Creeping up to the door, Lassiter took a deep breath. Then he lashed out with his right foot. The door crashed inward, revealing two startled faces.

The man called Sam had a thick down-curving mustache. His right hand flicked toward a holstered gun, but Lassiter quick-thumbed a shot an inch from his fingers and into the wall to make him change his mind.

"Lassiter," he breathed, recognizing him. "Don't try nothin', Pinky."

Pinky, with hair a shade of pale strawberry and a darker beard, stood clutching an empty pan, as if toying with the idea of hurling it into Lassiter's face. Hearing the name Lassiter froze him for a moment. Then he nervously placed the pan on a rickety table and lifted his hands. In the cramped quarters, there was only room for the table, two chairs, two bunks and a stove. The lower right-hand corner of a window had been broken, a rag stuffed into the opening.

"There were five of you," Lassiter said tensely. "Where'd the other three go?"

"Don't know nothin' about nobody else," Sam Benley said with a straight face.

"I'm talking about the ones who helped you move the cattle." Lassiter mentioned the hundred head of K-27 beef, the twenty-five head belonging to DL.

The two men exchanged glances, a possible lie floating between them. Lassiter seized on it.

"I want the truth, damn it."

"Don't know nothin' about no cows," Pinky said.

Lassiter gave a harsh laugh. "You and your friends put me to a lot of extra riding today. You thinned down cows I've been fattening up. I want an answer!"

Something in his voice caused them to study him more closely, their eyes on his tight, dark face. Then Sam Benley's shoulders sagged and he began to talk. He said their companions had gone back to ranch headquarters.

"The ranch meaning Hayfork?" Lassiter asked angrily.

"Yeah, but me an' Pinky work for Doc Plane's Rafter 2."

"Whose idea was this, anyhow?" Lassiter demanded.

"You see, Rudd figured chasin' them cows would keep you busy an' you'd likely give the Kerrington gal a hand."

"For what reason?" Lassiter snapped.

Sam Benley looked worried. "Don't git mad at us.

We only do what we're told." He was nervously eyeing Lassiter's gun, a weapon pointed at his midriff.

Pinky Dobbs sank to one of the chairs as if his spindly legs refused to support his weight any longer. "What you aim to do with us, Lassiter?" he managed in a squeaky voice.

"I figure to turn you over to McBride. We'll see what our estimable sheriff does with a rustling charge against Hayfork and Rafter 2. I'm sure Miss Kerrington will go along with me on it."

Sam Benley got a wise look on his face. "McBride's busy this week . . . with the trial."

"What trial?" Lassiter's eyes narrowed.

"That gal out at Apperson's—Ruthie. Rudd claims she killed her partner, Pete Shamrock."

A sudden chill lodged in the pit of Lassiter's stomach. "He died of a broken neck."

"Looks like she done him in, is the way I heard it," Sam Benley persisted. "Shot him in the back of the head." While Lassiter stared coldly, trying to digest it, the man continued, "That's why Rudd wanted you busy for a few days. He figured it'd take you that long to run down them cows. But you done it purty quick, I admit. Quicker'n Rudd expected, for sure."

"You mean Ruthie's been *arrested?*" Lassiter demanded.

Benley's stubby fingers played with an end of his thick mustache. "Circuit judge is due in Wayfield. Trial won't take more'n a day, so Rudd claims."

"Well, I'll be damned," Lassiter said under his breath. "I turn my back for a few days and look what happens."

He made an instant decision, forgetting any thought

of taking the pair in on a rustling charge. That could come later.

"Lie face down on the floor. Both of you. *Now!*"

They grumbled protests but finally did as ordered. Lassiter quickly disarmed them. He found a rawhide string and ran this through the trigger guards of two rifles and revolvers. He carried the weapons outside, then lifted the bars of the corral, freeing the two horses. They went scampering down a long slope of shale, raising dust.

"I'll leave your guns a mile or so down the trail," Lassiter told the two scowling men in the doorway. Just to be sure, he made it nearly two miles before dropping the weapons.

Then he put spurs to his black horse and turned in the direction of Apperson's. He wanted a conference with Owney Devlin.

It was after three hours of fast riding that Lassiter reached Apperson's. His horse needed water and oats. He paid a roustabout to take care of the animal, then entered the big barnlike establishment. It was too early for a crowd to have gathered. Drink in hand, Lassiter walked over to the piano on a raised platform where one-eyed Apperson was running a few chords.

"How's Devlin?" he asked the owner.

"As usual," Apperson said with a dry laugh. "At least he was last night."

"Is it true about Ruthie?" Lassiter asked, watching the man's good eye, the other hidden by a black patch.

"Poor kid, but there was nothin' I could do."

"What do you mean, nothing you could do?"

"First place, I can't buck the sheriff. Not in my

business, I can't. Besides, the deck is stacked against her." Apperson emphasized his displeasure by hitting a discordant chord on the piano.

"Deck stacked against her? Just how?"

"Main witness against her will be Eddie Pyne."

"That bastard."

"Circuit judge ain't due for a day or so, I hear. . . ."

Lassiter didn't wait to hear more and headed for the shack where Devlin had been living.

17

THAT MORNING RUTHIE HADN'T eaten the breakfast
that was brought to her. The thought of food nauseated
her, but she did drink a little coffee. That this was
happening to her was unbelievable. She saw faces
watching her from the alley where the blanket draped
over the window had caught on one of the bars. But
she was too weary and upset to straighten it out. Let
them look, she thought in her despondency.

The Wayfield Furniture Store had been transformed
into a makeshift courtroom; the regular courthouse
had burned down earlier in the year. Most of the stock
had been transferred to a storehouse. Counters had
been pushed back against shelving, with chairs for jury
and spectators brought in from the church. A scarred
desk served as a bench for Judge Silas Quincy. A tall,
Lincolnesque type of man, he early disposed of the
three pending court cases and at present was over at
the Four Aces with Sheriff McBride, having an early
whiskey.

"Clears out the pipes," he told the assemblage with a wink. "Seems I'll have a lot of talkin' to do today."

"Shouldn't take long, Judge," Joe Rudd spoke up. "She's guilty as hell. That right, Eddie?" Eddie Pyne, wearing his one good suit, bobbed his head but failed to meet Rudd's eyes.

"Guilty as hell," he agreed.

"We'll see," said Judge Quincy jovially. He nudged Vince McBride who stood beside him in the early morning crowd, dressed up in a black suit, his badge glittering on his vest. Since assuming the office of sheriff last year he had put on so much weight from so much free food and whiskey that he could no longer button the coat. "Vince, have you ever hung a female?" the judge wanted to know.

McBride swallowed, looked a little sick and said, "No . . . no, I ain't never, Judge."

"You might get a little practice in," the judge said loudly and with a wink, which brought on a torrent of laughter. But it did nothing to ease the pained expression on McBride's corpulent features.

The jury had already been selected and stood at the far end of the bar being served free whiskey by Cavendish, the owner, because of the civic duty they were about to perform.

"I don't want any of you fellas drunk," Judge Quincy called across the crowded saloon.

"We won't be, Judge," Elk Raffelson, who had been chosen foreman, shouted. He lifted a glass high and the judge raised his in a toast.

"Here's to gettin' the job done quick so I can catch the four o'clock stage outa here," the judge said. "Got a heavy schedule over in the next county."

"Amen," Rudd put in and drank. He bought a round of drinks for the house.

Presently they all trooped over to the store. The judge removed his hat, sat down behind the desk and rapped for silence with the gavel that always traveled with him. Only a sprinkling of women sat in the few seats; most of the onlookers were standing along three of the walls, some sitting on counters.

For the most part, the women had come to see up close the soiled dove on trial for her life. A hush fell over the big room when Ruthie was ushered in. The lawyer appointed to defend her edged his chair away when she sat down. She was wearing a rather flamboyant blue dress that had been brought from Apperson's.

Judge Quincy proclaimed that court was in session and that they were to proceed to the business of the day.

The prosecutor, a dour man who shook a thin forefinger in Ruthie's face most of the time, pranced up and down in front of the jury, explaining the various points he wanted to get across. The jury generally looked bored. One of them was asleep and had to be nudged awake by the juror next to him.

When Ruthie took the stand, the big room quieted. She nervously explained how she and Pete Shamrock had gotten lost on the old road and how he had lost his temper and beaten her. And then, nearing the bottom of the grade, the wagon had struck a deep rut and overturned. Both of them had been thrown out, but she had survived.

"When he lay in the road unconscious, you fired a bullet into the back of his head," the prosecutor accused.

"Oh, no . . ." Ruthie was horrified.

Eddie Pyne was called to the stand. He said that one night he shared Ruthie's blankets, acting embarrassed as he told it. There were a few titters from male onlookers; the women sat rigid in their chairs.

"She confessed that she killed him," Eddie said, his eyes pointed toward the ceiling.

"That's a lie!" Ruthie cried. "You were . . . were never in my blankets and I never confessed such a thing."

Judge Quincy restored order by hammering with his gavel. Eddie was directed to proceed.

"I told Mr. Rudd about it an' he was . . . he was . . ." Eddie groped for the right word and flashed Rudd an imploring look. Rudd mouthed the word and Eddie said, "We was both appalled . . . appalled, that's what we was."

It was obvious to any objective viewer of the proceedings that the witness had been coached. Eddie told about digging up the corpse, finding the bullet hole and bringing the body to town where charges were filed.

"It's time for you good men and true," Judge Quincy said to the jury, "to take a look at the deceased."

Some of them said they had already seen it, but the judge was firm on that point. One by one, with handkerchiefs to their nostrils, they passed the coffin where the deceased lay face down and saw the bullet hole in the back of the skull.

They filed back into the store and took their seats. The defense attorney, looking annoyed, got up and asked the jury for mercy for his client, suggesting imprisonment for twenty years instead of execution.

"But I didn't do it!" Ruthie cried.

And the defense attorney relayed it to the jury. "She says she didn't do it."

Judge Quincy rapped for silence. There was a general clearing of throats. Ruthie, looking pale and frightened, sat tensely.

The judge asked if the jury had reached a verdict. Elk Raffelson, the foreman, a thin man with a prominent nose and bushy eyebrows, said, "We already voted her guilty!"

He sat down quickly.

Judge Quincy looked at his watch. It was a quarter to four, about fifteen minutes before the stage was due in town. He would be on it, heading north. He intended to have no part in the spectacle that was shaping up. Judge Quincy had never before condemned a female, but he managed to look stern. He told Ruthie to stand up, which she did, visibly shaking.

"Poor thing," Irma Heathcott said in the quiet courtroom, and several women nodded their heads in agreement. Judge Quincy frowned at Ruthie.

"For the willful act of murdering the man known as Peter Shamrock," the judge intoned, "I hereby sentence you to hang by the neck until you are dead." And then into the stillness that followed, "And may God have mercy on your soul."

Ruthie seemed to be in a state of shock as she was led quickly from the courtroom by Sheriff McBride who seemed anxious to get away.

Mary Taleson was on her feet. She was a sprightly, dark-haired woman who owned the store with her husband Josh. "Just a minute, Judge. It seems to me the jury brought in a verdict awful soon." She turned and looked scornfully at the jurors now filing out of the building. "Likely the proceedings were cut short so they could get back to their bottles at the Four Aces," Mary Taleson said loudly. "I don't think the lady had a fair trial."

"She had as fair a trial as this territory will ever give her," the judge said, his temper beginning to slip.

Another woman was on her feet. "I agree with Mary." And this prodded several men to add their voices.

Bert Jenkins of the livery stable said, "The only evidence you had was what that young fella gave." He turned his round head on a spindly neck till he saw Eddie Pyne trying to slip out a side door. "Him, I mean."

This caused Eddie to scamper across the wide turnaround for wagons next to the store, and then over to the Four Aces.

There was a muttering as protestors gathered around Mary Taleson's slight figure, her dark hair with wisps of gray gathered under a small bonnet.

"It's a disgrace, that's what it is!" she shouted, waving her small fists in the air. "We should all write the territorial governor and let him know what's going on over here."

"Amen to that," agreed her heavyset husband. Sunlight was reflected on his eyeglasses. "All we heard was Eddie Pyne say she shot the fella. An' she claims she didn't."

"I wouldn't take much stock in the word of a man who goes behind his uncle's back," another woman spoke up, "and takes as his wife the woman the uncle was figurin' to marry." There was a murmur of approval.

At the Four Aces, Judge Quincy, one eye on his watch, the other on a front window to watch for the stagecoach, had a suggestion to make.

"I say the sooner you get the job done, the better."

"We don't even have a gallows," Vince McBride moaned. "It burnt when the courthouse did."

"Take her out of town," the judge whispered. "The biddies in town are already stirring up trouble." He nodded his head at three of them seen through a window, standing stiff-backed in front of the Wayfield House.

"How about the old Rubio Mine," Rudd said. "There was plenty of shoring left last time I was out there. Hang her from a timber."

That seemed like a good idea to those in on the scheme.

Rudd turned to a pale-faced Eddie Pyne. "Buck up, Eddie," Rudd said, giving him a whack on the shoulders. "You told the truth today and that's all anybody can do."

Eddie gave a sick smile and said, "The truth. Yeah, I told it all."

18

BECAUSE OF THE LATE hour, Lassiter had spent the night at the shack Devlin shared with Ruthie. Devlin was in no shape to digest any information. Lassiter managed to get some food into him but directly after the meal, Devlin passed out.

In the morning, Lassiter got Devlin dressed, then pushed a cup of steaming black coffee in front of his red-eyed former partner slumped at the table.

Devlin's hand shook when he raised the cup. Spilled coffee made a puddle on the table top, but he did get some of it down.

"Tell me again," Devlin mumbled, "about the trouble Ruthie's in. I didn't hear you so good the first time."

Straddling a chair, Lassiter told him in crisp tones. "It's up to us to see that she comes out of this all right."

"So somebody fired a bullet into the back of that fella's head. An' they claim Ruthie done it, eh?"

"Which means somebody's lying," Lassiter added grimly.

"When I find out who it is . . ." Devlin's large hands closed into fists. During his drinking bout he had lost weight. Flesh hung on his large frame. He looked gaunt. But he had shaved his beard. On his thin face were numerous cuts where his shaking hand had invited slices from the razor.

"One drink," Devlin said, "that's all, just one." Lassiter regarded him coldly. "I need it bad, Lassiter," Devlin said.

"Just one, remember."

Devlin reached out for a half-filled bottle and slopped some whiskey into his coffee. He finished it quickly and stood up. "Ready as I'll ever be," he said with a broken laugh.

After a night of rest, Lassiter's black horse was revived, ready to hit the trail. But for the first few miles Lassiter had to ride easy because Devlin swore his head would come loose and roll if his horse loped. But the gravity of Ruthie's predicament plus the coffee and the shot of whiskey seemed to settle him down. They increased their speed.

To Lassiter, it seemed an interminable journey. Finally, in the clear light, they saw Wayfield's lumpy buildings snug against the dun-colored terrain. A few wisps of smoke here and there attested to the fact that pots were on the fire. Life goes on, Lassiter thought as they entered town. He was surprised when a glance through a front window of the Four Aces showed the place to be practically deserted.

But he didn't want to go over and make inquiries where whiskey was too handy for Devlin. "We'll see Ruthie first off," Lassiter said.

They swung toward the sheriff's office and the jail

behind it. But the office was locked. When they went around to the alley and peered through a barred window into a cell, all they saw was a drunk. He was curled up, not on a bunk, but on the floor.

The window of the adjoining cell had been covered with a blanket, but one corner was caught in the bars. Stooping, Lassiter peered in. He saw an unmade bunk and some empty dishes on a table. Over the back of a chair was a blue dress.

"Ruthie's," Devlin said in a tight voice at Lassiter's shoulder. "I've seen her wear it plenty of times."

Lassiter began to have a sick feeling in his gut. "Ruthie," he called softly through the window, thinking perhaps she might be out of his range of vision. But there was no reply.

"Go 'way," wailed the drunk in the adjoining cell. "I wanna sleep."

Two doors down was a saddle shop, but the door was locked. It was strange to be closed this time of day, Lassiter thought. It was midmorning. Then he wondered if it might be Sunday; sometimes he lost track of the days. But a swift count in his head told him it wasn't Sunday. However, the town did seem almost deserted.

From a corner of the building, Lassiter spotted activity at the Wayfield Store. "Come on," he beckoned to Devlin and hurried across the turnaround, taking two steps at a time to climb the loading platform.

The Talesons, with the assistance of four strong boys, were transforming the makeshift courtroom back into their store. Counters were being moved.

"You have any idea where we can find the sheriff?"

Lassiter asked Mrs. Taleson. With the sleeves of her dress rolled up, her jaw thrust out, she looked small but formidable. Her heavyset husband, coming in from the storeroom with a load of stock under his arm, gave her a slight shake of his head.

"I don't know where you can find him," Taleson said, avoiding Lassiter's eyes.

Lassiter assessed the situation. "You know, but you won't tell me," he guessed.

When the woman started to open her mouth, her husband said, "Mary, we got a business to run in this town. We don't want no more trouble than we got already."

"But, Josh . . ." she began.

"You already poked your nose in deep enough when you spoke up after the trial."

Lassiter's jaw dropped. "There's been a trial already?"

The woman nodded firmly. "Yes," she said.

"But out at Apperson's I was told the circuit judge wasn't due for another day or so . . ."

"He came in ahead of time," Josh Taleson said nervously.

His wife stiffened her back and said indignantly, "Eddie Pyne, he's the one . . ."

"What're you trying to say, ma'am?" Lassiter demanded.

"He gave testimony against her."

Josh Taleson set down his load of stock on a counter and got his wife by an arm. He whispered something in her ear. She went pale, then stalked into a hallway.

"I'm sorry," Taleson said, still avoiding their eyes, "but we got to live here."

Lassiter looked at the four boys who had paused in their chores to listen and stare, but Taleson took care of that. "Git back to work!" he said gruffly and they sprang to it.

Sensing they would get no information from them, Lassiter jerked his head at Devlin. He felt a sense of urgency as they started for the Four Aces—where he should have gone in the first place, he realized.

"Jeez, the trial's already been held," Devlin moaned, laboring to keep up with Lassiter's long-legged stride.

As they started past the veranda of the Wayfield House, Eloise came out of the hotel. She was wearing a drab brown dress and her blue eyes looked haunted.

Devlin spun around on the walk and glared up at her. She said in a faltering voice, "H—h—hello, Owney."

"Where's Eddie?" Devlin yelled. "Over at the store, the woman says he give testimony against Ruthie."

"He . . . he told about the bullet being fired into the man's head."

"There wasn't any bullet," Lassiter stated flatly.

"Oh, yes, but there is." She came forward a step, looking almost beautiful despite her attire. It must be tearing Devlin apart, Lassiter thought, to see her face to face again. But the only visible emotion on his friend's gaunt face was rage.

"How do you know there's a bullet?" Devlin demanded.

"The jury saw it. The body's at the undertaker's."

At that moment, Eddie Pyne sauntered from the Four Aces and started across the street. Then he saw his uncle and Lassiter talking with his wife and ducked back inside.

Lassiter spotted him. "There he is!"

Devlin started for the saloon doors, running erratically. Lassiter passed him and caught Eddie trying to slip out a side door. He flung him against the wall. Besides Eddie there were only Ed Cavendish and four customers in the place.

"That bullet, Eddie," Lassiter snarled, holding him against the wall. "I want to hear about it!" Eddie's eyes were wild, his mouth jerked. Lassiter repeated his question, slamming him against the wall again.

"You can see for yourself!" Eddie Pyne panted, trying to shout around the thick arm of Lassiter that was like a bar across his throat, pinning him against the wall. "I can prove it!" he cried, his voice half strangled.

Lassiter let him down. "Show me."

Cavendish even locked up the place and hurried to catch up with the others, a breeze fluffing out his oversized sideburns.

Walt Berryman, the little tub of an undertaker, was just climbing into the seat of a wagon.

"I ain't got time to talk business now!" he shouted, gathering in the reins. "Come back later."

Lassiter froze when he saw a coffin in the wagon. "Where're you heading, anyhow?" he demanded.

"All I know is I was told to be there by noon!"

But Lassiter barely heard him because Eddie Pyne was giving a triumphant yelp from inside the funeral parlor. "Here it is, Lassiter. Come have a look for yourself!"

A crowd was beginning to gather, attracted by the commotion.

"You wait," Lassiter told the undertaker and ran to where Eddie, a handkerchief held to his nostrils, had moved aside the lid of a coffin.

Lassiter held his breath and glanced in. There was indeed a bullet hole at the base of the skull. He slammed the lid down and fixed Eddie with a cold eye. Pyne blinked and looked away.

"You're always so goddamn smart!" Eddie Pyne's voice shook. "I wanted to prove you wrong for once."

"There was no bullet hole when I buried him," Lassiter said ominously, and all eyes flew to Eddie. But he didn't back down.

"You . . . you just never saw it is all," Eddie replied.

Mary Taleson came hurrying up from the store, lifting her skirts to keep them from dragging in the dirt. She was panting from her exertion, saying, "I don't care if my husband likes it or not. I'm sayin' it. They've took that poor girl out . . . to hang her!"

"She was found guilty by a jury," a gaunt man put in quickly.

Whether Devlin heard it or not, Lassiter never knew. But suddenly a great roaring burst from his throat and he lunged at his nephew. His backhand flew into Eddie Pyne's face with such force that it knocked him down.

He sat for a moment, blinking his eyes, blood running down over his chin from a smashed nose. Then he reached under his coat for a gun.

"Owney, look out!" Lassiter shouted. But Devlin was swarming all over the younger man, tearing away the gun. He threw it into the alley behind the funeral parlor. After hauling Eddie to his feet, he backhanded him again and again. Eddie cried out and fell to his knees.

"Owney!" It was Eloise's frantic voice barely heard above the tumult. "You'll kill him!"

But Devlin ignored her. He jerked his sobbing nephew erect, then shook him so hard that blood and sweat arced into the sunlight.

"Tell 'em you lied!" Devlin screamed. "Tell 'em all . . . *everybody!*"

"No, Uncle Owney . . ." Eddie Pyne was gasping for breath. Blood ran down his face, staining his shirt and coat. Devlin hit him again. Eddie's head jerked and he sagged as if about to go down again. But Devlin seized him by the arms, glaring into his face, ravaged even further as tears were mixed with the blood and sweat.

At last he broke down. "I lied . . . I lied . . . please don't hit me again."

Devlin thrust him away as if something too loathsome to touch.

"Then she ain't guilty after all," said a bystander in an awed voice.

"Where'd they take her?" Lassiter demanded of the man.

"I don't know. All we wanted was to be no part of it."

"He knows!" Mary Taleson pointed at the undertaker still frozen on the seat of his wagon.

"Rubio Mine!" he cried in a quavering voice. "I was s'posed to be there by noon. To . . . to pick up the body."

A glance at the sky showed Lassiter that the sun was nearing its zenith. "How far is it?" he demanded.

"Six, seven miles," the undertaker responded.

"How many are going with us!" Lassiter cried. Several men spoke up.

Devlin dragged his nephew along by an arm. As they ran for their horses, Lassiter had another glimpse of the coffin in the bed of the undertaker's wagon. He turned cold.

19

RUTHIE HAD AWAKENED EARLY that day. Her first thought was that she must find some way to get word to Owney Devlin, who in turn would get in touch with Lassiter. Between the two of them, she was confident, this terrible miscarriage of justice could be corrected. She was assured that she had plenty of time because when she mentioned it to the cook who brought her breakfast, he said, "Sure, ain't no hurry. They ain't even got a gallows built yet."

The use of the word made her cringe, but she was heartened to know there was time. However, she didn't see the wink that passed from the cook to Sheriff Vince McBride standing in the hall. He looked positively ill, with dark circles under eyes that seemed to have shrunken into his rather large skull.

After eating her breakfast, she actually felt better, her spirits lifting. Then they crashed to earth and splintered into a thousand pieces when two women were let into her cell and locked in.

"This is for you," a plump woman with jowls said, placing a black dress on her rumpled cot.

"What's that for?" Ruthie wondered aloud.

"More seemly for you to be wearin' black," said the second woman out of a thin mouth, "than the blue one." She gestured at the dress Ruthie was wearing.

"I don't understand. . . ." And then from the way the two women looked at her, rather shamefaced, she realized what it meant.

"But I thought . . ." Ruthie cleared her throat and tried again. "I thought I had several . . . days." She barely got out the last word.

"It's to be done at high noon," said the fat woman.

Ruthie rushed to the door, rattling it as she screamed, "Sheriff McBride, Sheriff McBride!"

But the sheriff didn't appear. The two women got her by the arms. "It's sad, I know," the thin one said, "but you brought it on yourself by puttin' a bullet in that fella's head."

"But I didn't, I didn't," Ruthie protested.

"You was found guilty by a jury an' sentenced by a judge!"

"Put on the dress, anyhow," urged the fat one.

She did change dresses behind a blanket held by the two women over the barred door to give her privacy. At least it took her mind off the coming terror. But her fingers were all thumbs and she had a hard time buttoning and unbuttoning. Once she had the dress on, the two women helped with the buttons. She was trembling so she could hardly stand.

"There'll only be a small crowd," said the fat woman. "You should be thankful for that. A lot of folks ain't goin' along with this."

"Don't go gettin' her hopes up, Doris," the thin woman put in sharply. "Too bad the reverend ain't in town."

"I reckon he was scared off after marryin' Owney Devlin's woman to his nephew."

"There'll likely be somebody out at the mine who'll read from the Scripture," the thin one said. "I better speak to Sheriff McBride about it."

The two women departed, leaving a forlorn Ruthie alone in the cell. Then she began thinking about her short life, unhappy for the most part. She had run away from home when she was twelve to escape a brutal stepfather. Then she had been found by Pete Shamrock. She wasn't ashamed of what she had done; it had been only a way to survive in the West. At first she had been excited being Pete Shamrock's girl. Then when his meanness began to show, it was too late and she became submissive. And now they were going to take her life for something she hadn't done. Oh, she had thought about killing Pete many times; but she lacked the nerve to do it. Besides, she had been taught that it was wrong to take a human life.

But they were going to take hers. She looked at the grim-faced men who surrounded her as they rode east out of Wayfield. At the edge of town, they passed through black cottonwoods and then a vast sea of sage. They began to climb a gradual slope. To the right was a great jumble of rocks against the base of a mountain that rose majestically into the azure sky. Never had a mountain looked more beautiful. High above, a great phalanx of wild birds streamed southward, and she knew that winter could not be far off—a season she would not live to experience. The thought of it brought a cold twinge across her shoulders.

They slipped through a belt of cedars and reached a bench where precipitous walls of granite rose skyward. Then there were ponderous, overhanging cliffs of yellowed sandstone.

She looked around at the faces of the horsemen. They had provided a sidesaddle for her, the ladies of Wayfield saying that in her black dress it would be most unseemly for her to ride astride.

She knew that her only chance was to appeal to the more sensitive ones in the group. She singled out an older man whom she sensed might be compassionate.

"I'm innocent," she said, her voice rough from her suppressed emotions. "I didn't kill him."

"You was judged fair an' square," the man said and spat tobacco juice through his white mustache.

She tried another and another. Either they looked away, refusing to meet her eyes, or reminded her that she was guilty.

She managed to maneuver her horse in beside Rudd's diminutive foreman. "I don't suppose there's any sense in appealing to a man like you," she said hopelessly. "I've heard of your reputation."

Dark eyes in the small face rolled up to meet hers. He started to speak and then Rudd intervened.

"You'd be wise to spend your time in prayer," he said sardonically to Ruthie, "rather than try to get sympathy. That right, Sid?"

But his foreman was staring back at some high rocks where the sheriff had disappeared.

"He's sick again," Salone said flatly.

"Seems we've got a sheriff with a spaghetti spine," Rudd said with a laugh and several others joined in.

Finally, a pale McBride caught up with them again, wiping his lips on the back of his hand. He looked even more haggard, Rudd decided, than Owney Devlin who had been living for some time with a whiskey bottle. McBride's broad face was peppered with beads of sweat.

"When I took this goddamn badge, I purely never figured I'd be asked to do what I got to do today." His corpulent figure vibrated in a shudder. "Oh my gawd . . ."

They rode under an arch of stone that bridged the canyon rim. Ahead was the dark green of oaks and the lighter shade of aspens, then the brilliant green of willows and cottonwoods in the center marching toward the far end of the valley.

"I'm appealing to you, Sheriff McBride," Ruthie said in a small voice that grew strong as she again pronounced her innocence.

"The judge sentenced you," McBride mumbled. "I got nothin' to do with it."

"You have . . . you could call off this . . . this farce!"

Tears rolled down her cheeks, which caused McBride to give her a nervous glance. "Now don't go gettin' yourself all upset."

"Why shouldn't I be upset? You're going to *kill* me!"

Her sobs caused some of the men to exchange awkward glances. A few like Joe Rudd were caught up in the excitement of it. The prospect of watching the sinful female lose her life was something that could be locked away in the mind, bringing it out for inspection during emotional peaks.

Rudd noticed the set of Salone's jaw, the scowl on his small face. "Cheer up, Sid, it's something to look forward to," he said jovially. But his foreman turned his head as he plodded along on a roan, such a coldness in the depths of his dark eyes that Rudd felt the impact clear to the base of his spine.

"I don't like the idea of killin' her," Salone said in a flat voice.

"*You* squeamish, Sid?" Rudd tried to laugh. "How many men have you killed anyhow?"

"Men, yeah. No women."

"Don't tell me you got ideas of rescuin' her," Rudd said with a broad smile so that Salone would know he was only joking.

Salone didn't reply. He was staring indifferently at a clump of silver spruces. A breeze blew a scent of sage into their faces.

Rudd turned in the saddle and studied Ruthie riding a few feet away. A delicate little morsel, no matter how often she'd been to the well with men. He wished now he'd made arrangements to spend last night with her. Maybe not in the jail but in a back room at the hotel. McBride could have managed it. The sight of her perched sidesaddle on a sorrel horse, her face streaked with tears, produced a familiar ache in him. But it was too late now to do anything about it, he realized after glancing around at the two dozen or so faces. There were Bible shouters among them who would hang a woman but be outraged at what they termed indecent conduct.

Well, anyway, today's work would put Owney Devlin in his place, Rudd reflected, and give Lassiter something to chew on. It was a way of getting even with them both—a pleasing thought on this bright day.

"Better hope there's somethin' left at the mine big enough for her to stand on," one of the men remarked.

"I reckon we should've put her in a wagon an' hauled out an empty beer barrel," said another, "for her to stand on."

"We'll find something at the mine," Rudd said confidently.

They only had another mile to go. The sun was creeping toward the point in the sky that passed morning into afternoon. A wind had come up, rustling the trees and moving great balls of clouds across the sky to give the day a steel-like brightness.

They reached a spring which gushed from the ground and went sweeping along a channel lined with willows. Here they pulled up to let the horses drink their fill. After all, they still had time; the judge had set the hour by yelling, "Make it noon," just before boarding the northbound stagecoach.

There was a sudden commotion of horses breaking away, a great surge of hoofbeats as Ruthie kicked her sorrel into a run. She lost the bonnet one of the ladies had pinned to her head, and her long hair streamed out.

"Get her!" Rudd yelled at Salone, but the little foreman was slow in getting his horse turned around.

Rudd swore and spurred his mount into a dead run. He caught up with her easily and brought her back, leading her horse. Being thwarted in her attempt to escape, she broke into another spate of tears.

"Out at Apperson's they say you want to get your hands on DL ranch!" she screamed at Rudd. "And that—"

"Who can believe what they hear at a place like Apperson's?" Rudd interrupted with a smile and looked around at the others.

"Be best all around if you made your peace with the Lord," the older man said to Ruthie, "so you can die with dignity, which I aim to do when my own time comes."

"Rudd will do anything to wreck Owney Devlin and Lassiter!" Ruthie cried, not swayed by the advice. "He . . . he's taking it out on me!"

They bunched their horses in close so she had no chance to make a run for it a second time.

"You coming, Vince?" Rudd shouted at a patch of willows.

McBride emerged, wiping his lips on a bandanna. He staggered to his horse like a ninety-year-old man and mounted up. He shuddered at the sight of Ruthie hunched in the sidesaddle, her face ravaged.

"I . . . I can't go through with it," he said in a shaking voice. "I purely can't. . . ."

"But you got to," one of the men said indignantly. "You're the sheriff. It's what you're being paid for."

"But I never thought this would be part of the job."

"If you're not up to it, Vince," Rudd said coldly, "we'll draw straws. That all right with you boys?"

Several of them shook their heads and said to leave them out of it.

"Then Sid will do it." Rudd stared at his foreman, seeking to punish him for the look the man had given him only a short time before.

No expression showed on Salone's small dark face. He only shrugged, which to most of them indicated that if necessary he'd take over the distasteful task.

"We should've taken time an' built a gallows in town," said the older man, sounding nervous.

"And have those biddies buttin' in?" Rudd said.

That quieted them down. They rode on, McBride with his eyes on the ground.

At last one of those in the lead sang out, "Here we are."

A faded sign—RUBIO MINE—dangled vertically from a length of rusted wire. The other wire had succumbed to weather.

They pulled up and some of them helped Ruthie from her high perch on the sidesaddle. She stood trembling on the ground, staring at the great hole in the side of a mountain. The mine opening was large enough to accommodate a big wagon with a high load.

The sheriff nudged Ruthie. "You get yourself some rest over by that tree yonder," McBride said, pointing. "Do some prayin'. It might help." His voice had smoothed out somewhat but was still ragged on the edges.

Ruthie walked over and sank to the ground in the shelter of pines. Wild roses clung to one wall of the abandoned mine. Scattered about were several pieces of rusted machinery, a hoist, some rails and an ore car. Several barrels were in various stages of disintegration.

Two men labored with a great block of wood. "She can stand on this," one of them said, panting.

"Be hard to kick out from under, though," Rudd said.

"Easy to tip it," one of them said.

Rudd and McBride and several others went over to inspect the hoist as a possible gallows, but it lay on its side and was in a sad state of disrepair. They decided on the block of wood and several of them worked it into the mine tunnel.

It seemed to Ruthie that her brain was numbed. She watched the proceedings from her plot of higher ground under the trees with her guards. She watched the large block of wood being placed under a thick beam, part of the mine shoring. One of the men produced a rope. He climbed up on the block of wood and fastened the rope around the beam and tied it securely, giving it a tug to make sure. Then he climbed down, cut off the rope at the desired length, then painstakingly began to fashion a hangman's noose.

She listened to some of the men talking about the mine. It was thought for a time that it was one of those that Coronado had been searching for back in the 1500s, one worked by the Apaches. But soon the vein of ore petered out and the mine closed down. A lot of investors lost money.

The story was long-winded. Rudd looked annoyed. Finally he pointed at the sky. "It's noon."

The sun was directly overhead.

"All right, Vince, she's all yours," Rudd said.

To Ruthie, it was as if they talked about someone else. She looked around, halfway expecting to see some poor soul who was condemned to death in this lonely place. But when a white-faced McBride came at a slow, staggering walk up the incline to where she was sitting, she realized she was the one they talked about. The sheriff held two short pieces of rope in his plump hand, his eyes agonized.

He halted in front of her, thick legs spread, and said, "I . . . I gotta tie your hands. Will you . . . you stand up?"

She remained seated, the figure of the sheriff swimming before her eyes.

It was Rudd who bent down, caught her under the arms and boosted her upright. Her knees almost caved in.

"Put your hands behind your back," McBride said in a hollow voice.

When she failed to respond, Rudd grabbed her arms and pulled her hands behind her back. "There you are, Vince."

She felt the bite of rope against bare skin.

"I reckon we better tie your ankles," McBride muttered and bent down.

She lacked the strength and coordination necessary to kick him in the face.

Finally, with Rudd on one elbow, the sheriff on the other, they carried her downslope and into the shadowed entrance of the mine. It smelled of dust and stale water, which lay in pools deeper in the tunnel. They boosted her up on the high block of wood. She wavered, nearly losing her balance, but they steadied her.

Two men made a step with their hands and boosted a third man high enough to place the noose about her neck and draw it tight.

"All right, Vince," Rudd said, "kick it out from under her."

"Oughta see if she's got any last
said in a voice barely audible. He
sweat. "Speak up," he said to R'
thing he uttered before he fell limply
in a dead faint. As the men stared at their ᵤ
sheriff, there was a sudden thunder of hoofbeats.

Rudd, who had been bending over the sheriff, stood
up. "The hell with Vince," he yelled. "Somebody kick
it out from under her!"

At that moment, he saw a horseman come pounding
out of the trees, gripping a rifle.

"Lassiter!" Rudd cried, standing stiffly.

20

ALL EYES SWUNG TOWARD the tall figure of Lassiter. The sight of his rifle made them cautious. "I came on ahead," he said thinly, sliding to the ground. "Looks like I'm in time."

Rudd was inching his hand along his belt, his eyes riveted on Lassiter's face.

"Rudd, if you even take a deep breath, you're dead," Lassiter warned.

In the sudden stillness, Rudd said, "You've got no business bustin' in here." More hoofbeats indicated riders approaching. "The sheriff has fainted and . . ."

"We've got something for you boys to hear!" The hoofbeats soon materialized into mounted men reining in under the trees. "Some of you cut Ruthie down," Lassiter shouted.

Three of them sprang forward and cut the rope. Ruthie's knees trembled as she was helped down from the block of wood.

By then, a bloodied Eddie Pyne had been shoved

forward by his red-eyed uncle. "Speak up, Eddie," Devlin snarled.

Eddie cast a fearful glance at a glowering Joe Rudd. Then, as if deciding Rudd was less of a threat than his uncle and Lassiter, he began to talk. "I . . . I lied. Shamrock never had a bullet in his head when he was dug up. It was done afterward."

"Who fired the gun, Eddie?" Devlin demanded.

Eddie Pyne's voice was so low that Devlin made him repeat it. "Salone! Sid *Salone!*"

Most eyes swung to Salone whose small dark face was unreadable. Only the black eyes were alive, lancing into the face of a terrified Eddie.

Rudd gave a hoot of laughter. "Now Eddie is lying, for sure. My foreman never fired a bullet into that hombre's head. The bullet was already there."

"Eddie says no. I say no." Lassiter stepped into a pool of sunlight, the rifle pointed at Rudd's breastbone. "This range has had about enough of you."

This brought an angry murmur from most of the men.

Sheriff McBride had revived, looking shamefaced for having fainted. Then he was told what had happened, that Ruthie was cleared; Eddie Pyne had lied in court.

"Thank God," McBride murmured shakily.

Ruthie was sobbing in Devlin's arms.

"I'm gonna marry her," Devlin said belligerently as if daring anyone to contradict him. His eyes settled on Lassiter. "An' I'll never take another drink as long as I live."

"I hope so, Owney," Lassiter said.

Men crowded around to offer congratulations on the coming wedding. They removed their hats and spoke softly to Ruthie, a woman they had intended to hang only minutes before.

Rudd, his foreman and less than half of the party rode away at a gallop in the direction of town.

On the way back, Lassiter rode beside Devlin who was talking about the future with Ruthie. "After we marry, we'll go away . . ."

"But, Owney, your life is here . . . at DL."

"I done cut that outa my life."

"You can't just hand it over to Eddie."

"I'm doin' it for my sister Rose, not for Eddie."

"Even after he nearly led Ruthie to the gallows?"

"For Rose only. I done told you, Lassiter."

"Forget your dead sister for once!" Lassiter knew he had said the wrong thing; Devlin glowered. "I'll tell you one thing," Lassiter said, "Ruthie'll make you a good wife."

"I'm countin' on it."

Ruthie, riding on the far side of Devlin, made no comment. She had recovered some of her color, but fear was still mirrored in her eyes.

Eddie had ridden away by himself on a borrowed horse.

"With your new plans, Owney, you've got to get back on DL," Lassiter said, trying again.

But Devlin shook his head.

"Don't be so damn stubborn." Lassiter's nerves had been filed thin by all that had happened. It had been a bad day all around. The least of it was that the enmity between himself and Joe Rudd had deepened.

He could live with that; he could even see some good in Devlin and Ruthie getting married. But Devlin's refusal to take his rightful place at DL raised his temper.

"Of my own free will I gave Eddie a quit-claim deed to my half of the ranch," Devlin was saying. "The least I can do for the memory of his ma is to stay put."

"Forget the memory of his mother. Think of yourself, of Ruthie."

"I done said all I'm gonna say, Lassiter."

"How do you figure to earn a living?" Lassiter demanded. "As your wife, Ruthie can't . . . well, go on as she was."

"Damn right she won't. She'll stay home. I'll earn us a livin'. Don't worry none about that."

"Look, I'll put in a few hundred dollars if you will. Give it to Eddie. Eloise told me once she almost wished she'd never left St. Louis. Chances are, they won't want to go back there on account of the fella Eddie killed in Missouri. But they could go farther West. Frisco, maybe."

Devlin rode for over a mile without saying anything. Then finally he responded. "I'll think it over, Lassiter."

This was heartening to Lassiter. At least he had made some progress, however slight, on this memorable day.

"I want to give you two a wedding present ahead of time," Lassiter said. "I'm paying for a room at the hotel for a couple of nights. You both deserve it."

Devlin thought that over, then leaned over in the

saddle and whispered to Ruthie. She nodded her head. Devlin looked around. "I'll let you do it, Lassiter. But it's got to be a loan. Understand?"

"Owney, for Christ's sake . . ." Then he caught himself and shrugged. "All right, a loan it is."

Some of the Wayfield ladies, having for the most part been indignant at Ruthie's hasty trial and sentencing, refused to unbend when it came to socializing. Others, including Mary Taleson, called Ruthie and Devlin into the Wayfield Store.

"Rudd an' that Eddie Pyne oughta stand trial for tryin' to murder this poor gal," she said. "An' that's what it amounts to!"

Other women and several men in the store voiced their agreement. "We've got to have a talk with McBride an' have him arrest them two scalawags," spoke up a gray-bearded man, shaking a fist.

But at the hotel where several families were dining, Ruthie received another type of reaction.

"Don't look at her," a mother hissed to her small son.

"Why not, Mama?" asked his round-eyed sister.

Ruthie shivered. She had changed from the hideous black dress back into her blue one, which lifted her spirits to a point. But now she wished they'd gone straight home instead of accepting Lassiter's offer of a hotel room.

"The way that female is treatin' you, boils my temper," Devlin growled as he buttered a slice of bread.

"I'm used to it, Owney, Lord knows."

"Well, you shouldn't be. Her an' some of the others was all for you when they thought you was gonna be hung. But now they've turned on you."

"I guess you can't blame them," Ruthie said, spooning her soup. "My life has been so different from theirs."

Allie Kerrington entered the dining room, wearing a green dress to match her eyes. It was Lassiter's favorite. She looked around, hoping to see the familiar dark face. When she didn't, there was disappointment in her eyes. Then she saw Devlin dining with the young lady who had lived with terror that day. Allie crossed the room, her heels clicking.

"Thank God things didn't turn out as some people had planned," she said earnestly to Ruthie. "I intend to write Judge Chalmers at the territorial capital and insist some action be taken against Rudd and Pyne for their conspiracy."

"Thanks," Ruthie said with a strained smile, "but from what I hear, Rudd has too much political power around here."

"We'll see about that." Allie cleared her throat. "Did . . . did Lassiter stay in town, do you know?"

"He went home," Devlin said.

Allie thanked him and took a table by herself. It was disappointing to learn that Lassiter had gone back to DL. She had hoped to be able to thank him for finding her rustled cattle, which had been driven into the mountains and abandoned. Obviously, Rudd was behind it, hoping to keep them from possibly interfering in his plans for Ruthie. The man was despicable and neither he nor Pyne should go unpunished.

When she had given her order to Len Crandall, who was waiting on tables that evening, she found herself studying Ruthie across the room. Ruthie seemed quite young and was rather attractive in a brassy sort of way. Rudd had been instrumental in trying to send her to the gallows, everyone was saying.

But Rudd, as usual, was carrying it off well. She heard that he was across the street, drinking with his cronies, with no one—at least in the Four Aces— apparently holding anything against him.

As she was finishing her soup, Devlin came over to her table. She hadn't realized how big he was.

"Miss Kerrington," he began awkwardly, "I was thinkin' maybe you could use a hand out at your place."

"You're speaking for yourself?"

"Yes, ma'am."

Allie debated, flicked a glance at Devlin's table companion and through her mind flashed all the things she had heard about the girl. The least of which was her immoral association with Devlin. Did she want such a woman living on the ranch? Then one side of her thought it was mean of her.

"I could bust horses," Devlin said. "I'm good at that."

Silently, she thanked him for settling the matter for her. He was, after all, Lassiter's ex-partner. And she didn't want to offend Lassiter by turning Devlin down cold. But breaking horses would be temporary work and wouldn't require a companion such as Ruthie to live on the ranch. And she wouldn't suggest it.

"I do have some horses that need breaking," Allie said, smiling up at his broad face. "And others that need some touching up." She named a figure; Devlin accepted.

He thanked her and returned to his table. Allie saw him say something to the girl, smile and pat her hand. He cares for her, she thought. He really does. But she wondered how a woman who had given to so many could channel her love to one man.

She knew it was cruel of her not to offer him a steady job and let Ruthie live there. Over the years, they had built quarters for the few married riders carried on the K-27 payroll. Why would it hurt to let Devlin and the woman have one of them? But she knew what it was—her stiff-necked morality. Thinking about it, she almost laughed. Here she was, an unmarried female who had spent two nights with Lassiter and she talked about morality.

Yes, she could have given Devlin a job as rider. Not foreman, however, for she still hoped to lure Lassiter into that job. But she realized Lassiter's arguments against it. He was determined to see that Devlin took his rightful place at DL and kicked the nephew out. But Eddie Pyne had the law on his side, a little matter Lassiter seemed to forget. He possessed the quit-claim deed Devlin had signed.

She must point this out to Lassiter more forcibly the next time they were together. When he finally realized the logic of her argument, he would be only too glad to come in with her as foreman. And after that, something deeper, more permanent, could develop.

She visualized their wedding announcement in the frontier papers: Allie and Lassiter Lassiter, at home. It was the only way she could think to put it because she didn't know Lassiter's first name. She had once asked him if he didn't have a given name and he'd only offered her his familiar wry grin and said nothing. He was truly a man of mystery.

The Pynes rode five miles out of Wayfield in the ranch wagon, the one they had intended to carry them to Prescott on their wedding night. Their weariness had caused them to seek a bed at Apperson's.

Eloise shuddered as she thought back on that horrible night when Devlin had dragged her across the bed so that staring eyes banked in the doorway could see every exposed inch of her. Her cheeks stung in memory of the shame. This was compounded by her husband's confession today of lying; it had nearly sent a woman to her death.

"You act like you blame me!" The first words Eddie Pyne had spoken to his wife. His white-knuckled hands gripped the reins. His lips were so cut and swollen from the backhands given him by his uncle that she could barely understand him.

"You shouldn't have lied." She clung to a seat brace to keep from being pitched out onto the uneven road. Eddie was driving much too fast, too recklessly. They were crossing the low swell of a slope fringed with trees, then downward where the sun burst over a rim, filling the shadowed canyon with light.

"You act like you *hate* me!" Eddie cried.

"I hate no one, Eddie. Will you please slow down? You're pushing those horses much too fast."

"I'll slow down when I feel like it."

A white hawk sailed out of some trees and swept across the road. Shading her eyes, she watched it a moment, envying its freedom. Below the hawk was the

pounding team, the jolting wagon and the pale woman.
Miles of sage stretched toward the mountains.

"Goddamn that Lassiter!" Eddie exploded. "He's
the one who put my uncle up to makin' a fool of me in
front of everybody!"

"Would it have been better to have let the woman
hang?"

"They'd have never hung her," he said confidently.
"At the last minute they'd have let her go."

"I don't think so."

"Oh, you don't, huh?" Wrapping the reins around
his left hand, he made a threatening gesture with his
right. "You keep on and you'll get a backhand."

"You ever hit me, Eddie, and we're through."

"Go back to St. Louis an' good riddance."

"Oh, no. I'm a partner in DL Ranch. I have no
intention of leaving."

He turned in the seat to stare at her. Finally, he
slowed the team.

"That's better," she said, and absently beat dust out
of her skirt.

What she had said about not leaving DL had made a
profound impression on him. He didn't know quite
where he stood in the matter.

When they got home, he was grumpy to the men and
ordered Upshaw to put the team and wagon away.
Then he seized Eloise by the arm and walked her to
the house.

He heated water for himself, dragged a tub into the
kitchen and had a bath. No longer wearing his bloodied and torn shirt and with his face washed, he looked
almost human. But there were still swellings and abrasions from the beating his uncle had given him.

In silence, Eloise heated up some leftovers for a meal. Finally, Eddie's temper began to shred. "Ain't you even gonna talk to me?" he whined.

"Not until you say you're sorry that you lied. And are glad that poor girl didn't die."

"Holy Jeezus!"

When Eloise went to bed, Eddie started to join her. But she turned on her stomach. "Either you sleep on the sofa in the parlor or I will."

"I got my rights . . . I'm your *husband.*"

"You have no rights until you become a man and own up to being sorry for what you did."

He stalked off to the parlor. But after midnight he woke her up and said he was sorry and begged forgiveness. Only then did she take him in her arms. But she felt nothing; the old magic was gone and she doubted if it would ever return. What he had done was despicable and even his begging to be forgiven had not lessened the sin as she thought it might.

She thought of Owney Devlin and tears filled her eyes. How could she have ever been such a blind fool?

21

Lassiter had tried many times to get Owney Devlin to return to DL Ranch without success. But at least he and Ruthie had left the shack at Apperson's and gone to live temporarily at K-27, where Devlin had contracted to break horses. Lassiter sensed that Allie was using cash she could ill afford, but admired her for the gesture. He had a feeling she had done it to please him.

But before the month was out the horse-breaking job came to an end. Devlin and Ruthie returned to the shack at Apperson's. But this time Ruthie worked there only as a waitress and sometimes as an entertainer. She danced and sang range songs in a reedy little voice that seemed to please the rough patronage. That she had declined to participate in her other activities displeased only a few at first who soon got over it, including Apperson himself.

Lassiter rode out to see them one day, halfway expecting to find his partner sleeping off last night's drunk. But Devlin, true to his word, had not touched a drop since he swore to Lassiter that he was through with whiskey.

"The Kerrington woman still hopes you'll come in with her," a clear-eyed Devlin said over coffee. "Sell out your half of DL to Joe Rudd. Eddie deserves him for a partner."

"We'll see."

"You could do worse than marry the gal." Devlin gave a tight smile.

"I've thought about it . . . some."

"But I guess it just ain't in you to settle down, is it, Lassiter?"

Lassiter gave Devlin back his smile, this one edged in bitterness.

Lassiter said he'd stop by and say hello to Ruthie on the way home. Devlin got his hat and said he'd go with him.

That afternoon the place was fairly crowded. Apperson was playing chords on the piano. There was a haze of tobacco smoke in the long-shadowed room. Being there with Devlin couldn't help but remind Lassiter of the terrible night when the nephew and his bride had been found together in bed.

"Eddie," Devlin said through his teeth, coming to an abrupt halt.

Lassiter looked in the direction of Devlin's stare and saw Ruthie standing near the piano, a set look on her face. And talking to her was Eddie Pyne.

Before Lassiter could stop him, Devlin rushed across the room and seized him by an arm. Ruthie started to protest, but Devlin told her to keep out of it. Devlin dragged his nephew outside.

"Stay away from Ruthie!" Devlin thundered as Lassiter stepped outside.

"Uncle Owney, I only wanted—"

But his uncle cut him off, sneering, "How about that killin' back in Missouri? Maybe you lied about that too!"

"No, I never, Uncle Owney . . ."

Devlin got him under the arms and pulled his pale face up even with his enraged one. Eddie's feet dangled in the air. "Tell me again how it happened!" Devlin demanded.

Eddie, obviously frightened of being beaten again, had a time getting it out. "Like I told you already, Uncle Owney," he said finally, "it was the day after my aunt's funeral an' I asked this gal to go to the school dance. But Clyde Kaney asked her too. An' he got mad an' called me out. Hell, I admit I was scared, 'cause the Kaneys had a bad rep. But we met out in a bunch of trees like he wanted an' I . . . I just got lucky. I killed him."

"And then you ran."

"The Kaneys wouldn't figure it was a fair fight, which it was."

"How would they figure it? That you cheated some way, likely."

"But I didn't cheat, Uncle Owney. Honest to God."

"I wouldn't believe a damn word you said, anyhow. Not after you lyin' about Ruthie." He set his nephew back on his feet and jerked his thumb. "Go on, get the hell outa here. Don't come back."

"But, Uncle Owney . . ."

Devlin made a threatening gesture. "You heard me."

Eddie started backing up. Patrons had come to the door to stare. "Eloise talked me into comin' over . . . an' apologizin' to Ruthie. . . ."

Then he whirled, got his horse and spurred south toward DL.

"I don't believe a damn word of it," Devlin snarled.

But later Ruthie confirmed it.

Lassiter was thoughtful as he rode home. In the distance, sunlight touched dark blue lines of canyons and rock walls. There the sage had lost color and in the late-afternoon light became a long grayish slope that ended at uprearing granite walls. He came to the rim of a low escarpment and drew rein, looking around. Down below, a pronghorn loped across the flats. He saw a jack rabbit and to his left two deer bounding toward some cedars.

He could see where drifting cattle in single file had trampled through high grass to leave a twisting trail as if made by a giant snake.

As he sat in his saddle, he fashioned and lit a cigarette, drawing the smoke deep into his lungs. He wore a half smile as he thought of Devlin's remark: "It just ain't in you to settle down. . . ."

For the first time in his life, Lassiter had tried mightily to put down roots. From the first it had been a disaster—Devlin acknowledging sheepishly that his eye had caught the picture of a pretty girl in a catalogue that someone had discarded in a saloon. And he had written her and after a brief correspondence had been accepted. And on top of that revelation came Devlin's declaration that he had thought of marriage to provide a home for his young nephew then living back in Missouri. Only as it turned out the nephew hadn't proved to be as young as his uncle had thought, having lost track of time over the years. The nephew had arrived unannounced, ending up marrying his uncle's intended picture bride.

Lassiter had always avoided settling down permanently in one place, making the one commitment many women had wanted but which he was reluctant to give. He supposed it stemmed from his childhood, never having known his mother who had died shortly after his birth.

Early in life he had acquired a love of books, introduced by a former schoolteacher he had worked with as a boy. Lassiter had read everything he could get his hands on. His early years had been stormy, but with maturity there were more ups than downs. Instinctively, he shied away from putting down roots. His own father had put them down and lost his wife, Lassiter's mother.

And here on Diablo range, he had intended to put down his own roots, at long last. Since the day he had made that decision, nothing had gone right.

That day when he reached DL he learned from Eloise that Eddie had ridden to Hayfork to seek Joe Rudd's counsel. He intended to spend the night.

"I wish he'd stay away from that man," Eloise said worriedly.

That evening Lassiter cleaned his weapons. With Eddie getting cozy again with Joe Rudd, he could expect trouble.

Shortly past midnight, Lassiter was awakened by a sound in the yard. He quickly pulled on his trousers and went to the bunkhouse door.

"Stay put till I find out what it is," Lassiter hissed at

the white faces of his men, washed by pale moonlight from a side window.

Rifle in hand, he slipped out into the darkness. Cicadas started making a minor racket in the trees. An owl hooted. Moonlight fell on distant peaks like a splash of silver.

In the barn, a man was unsaddling by lantern light. It was Eddie Pyne. Lassiter entered the barn, scowling.

"I heard you figured to spend the night at Hayfork," Lassiter said.

The voice startled Eddie. He looked around, seeming distraught. "Rudd's changed. I dunno what's got into him. He wasn't friendly."

"Maybe he hasn't forgotten that you cheated him out of hanging Ruthie."

Memory of that day caused Eddie to lose color. He lifted off his saddle, placed it on the rack and drove his horse into the corral.

"You were seeking Rudd's counsel, is how I think your wife put it," Lassiter said, walking with him to the door.

"I . . . I wanted to ask him about my . . . my marriage."

"He's nobody to ask. What's he know about marriage?"

"Well, I thought . . ."

"You and Eloise having trouble?"

"I don't want to talk about it." Eddie Pyne stalked on through the moonlight, his walk no longer cocky. Lassiter heard him enter the house and close the door.

Lassiter returned to the bunkhouse and heard Tom Hefter's whispered advice. "If Eddie's makin' friends again with Joe Rudd, I'd watch my back trail if I was you."

"It's one reason I cleaned my guns."

Despite what Eddie had told him, Lassiter was not sure just how deep the friendship might be with Rudd. But he was taking no chances.

That night sleep did not come easily. His mind was filled with visions of Eddie and Rudd. And Owney Devlin and Ruthie. Not to mention Allie Kerrington—hers was the most vivid image of all.

22

THE FOLLOWING MORNING SID Salone appeared leading Rudd's saddled horse. Rudd, in fawnskin riding clothes, carrying a quirt, stood waiting on the veranda steps. He scowled as he thought about Eddie Pyne's visit yesterday.

"I was meanin' to ask you," Salone said when they were riding out, "did you ever hear from that fella back in Missouri?"

"Kaney? No, I never heard."

"Too bad."

"I mailed the letter way over a month ago. Either he didn't get it or he said to hell with it."

"That kind of knocks a hole in your plans, don't it?" the little foreman asked in his cold voice.

"We'll just have to think of something else is all," Rudd said shortly.

Being reminded of the letter was just one more irritation spawned by Eddie Pyne. The nerve of the little bastard riding out to Hayfork as if everything was forgiven for having opened his mouth to his uncle about that woman out at Apperson's. Not that it made much difference now. Any way you looked at it, Eddie Pyne's days at DL were numbered. Having received a reply to his letter to Jethro Kaney would have made for the grand finale which Rudd would have enjoyed. But now it would have to be done another way.

In Prescott, two male passengers among others alighted from the northbound stage. Jethro Kaney jerked a thumb at his cousin, Art. "Let's cut the dust with a little drinkin' whiskey."

"A helluva long ways to come, if you ask me," the younger Art Kaney muttered, looking around at the street crowded with rigs of all descriptions, the walks filled with pedestrians.

Balancing saddles on one shoulder, warbags on the other, they slouched along the walk to the nearest saloon. They were both big men with grim faces. Residents of the frontier settlement took one look at them and stepped aside.

They had a drink which Jethro paid for. Jethro engaged the bored barkeep in conversation, asking who had the cheapest saddlers for sale in the town.

The barkeep was tall, stooped, with thinning brown hair and a pale face that attested to his hours indoors out of the sun. He almost laughed and it was on the tip of his tongue to make a snide remark about a man in this rough country wanting cheap horses. When your life might very well depend on one. But Jethro Kaney's hard gray eyes locking with his changed his mind.

"Over at the A-1 Stables they got some cheap ones," the barkeep replied nervously.

The pair walked to the A-1 and there dickered for a sorrel and a bay. They got better mounts than their money afforded only because the stableman was afraid of them.

They saddled up and rode east.

The plump stableman pocketed his money and watched them go. His lips were dry. "Glad to see the last of those two," he confided to his hostler.

"Where they headin', anyhow?" the lank hostler asked, leaning on his pitchfork.

"Wayfield. I've got a hunch they'll bring trouble for somebody over that way."

Jethro Kaney was pushing forty, a man with a long face deeply webbed. His eyes were as hard and cold as winter stone. He had long arms and legs and a short torso. Art was not quite as tall and wore a surly look on a round face that bore a knife scar.

It was wild country they were crossing. Jethro kept one eye on the serrated points of the high rim splashed with sunlight, which the stableman had said they'd have to cross. They began to climb. Halfway up they avoided a gorge and kept going. On a shelf with clumps of aspens they had shade. They paused to rest. Jethro dismounted, grunting, and his boots rang on the stones. Insects hummed around his sweated face. Clouds rolled ponderously before the wind, with streaks of lightning followed by booming thunder.

Two days later, following a map that had been sent with the letter, they rode through a gate. Hayfork had been burned into the arch with a branding iron.

Sid Salone spotted them first and came pounding up with four of his men. They were spread out, gripping rifles.

Salone rode forward alone, his small dark face impassive. "Who might you be?" he asked the Kaneys in clipped tones.

Kaney looked the little man over, then introduced himself and his cousin. "Lookin' for a gent named Rudd."

Salone's thin lips broke into as much of a smile as he ever allowed himself. "Welcome to Hayfork, Mr. Kaney. Follow me." He led the way to the big house set in a grove of cottonwoods.

"Boss!" Salone shouted. "Company callin'."

Then he drew aside and motioned his men away.

Rudd came scowling down the porch steps, saw the animation on Salone's face and guessed the rest. He smiled. "You Kaney?" he asked the older of the pair.

"I am."

Art was introduced again. They shook hands all around.

"Took you long enough to get here," Rudd observed. "I'd about given you up."

"We was . . . out of the country." Then Jethro Kaney gave a short laugh. "In jail we was, to be exact."

This caused Rudd to chuckle. "Been there myself a few times," Rudd admitted as he took them into the house.

"We was put away for a year. Otherwise we'd have settled Eddie Pyne long before this. Where can we find the little bastard?"

"Patience, Jethro," Rudd said amiably. He gestured for them to take chairs. Art was looking around at low-beamed ceilings and paneled walls. The room was furnished with heavy Spanish pieces, long sofas, a big table and chairs.

Rudd removed a bottle and glasses from a large sideboard and sat down with them. He poured.

"My plan for Eddie Pyne includes two more gents." Rudd's voice hardened as he named them, Lassiter and Owney Devlin. The Kaneys drank whiskey and listened to Rudd expand on his grand plan.

In conclusion, he suggested they make themselves at home on Hayfork, but to stay under cover in case they had visitors.

"You followed my instructions to the letter so far," Rudd said, "about riding the stage to Prescott, then buying horses and riding the rest of the way. So let's follow through on the rest of it, eh?"

"You said somethin' about money," Jethro Kaney said from his slouched position in a big leather chair, his hooded eyes locked to Rudd's face.

"A thousand dollars . . ." Rudd's gaze slid from Jethro to Art with the scarred face. "A thousand dollars each," he amended, and the taciturn looks on the Kaneys broadened into smiles.

Rudd had decided in a flash that he could afford to be generous. Because the three thorns in his side would be eliminated once and for all.

Two days later, in Wayfield, Joe Rudd met Vince McBride in the latter's cubbyhole of an office in front of the jail.

"I got something to talk over with you, Vince," Rudd said pleasantly. "Let's take a ride."

Rudd turned for the door, expecting the sheriff to follow. But McBride stayed in his chair, his feet on the desk.

"You can tell me here," the sheriff said petulantly.

"What I got to say is private. I don't want any stray ears to come up sudden and hear what I'm saying."

Sheriff McBride scowled and thought about it, then heaved himself out of his chair. Rudd had stirred up enough votes to get McBride elected sheriff over a man named Ray Plunkett. Plunkett, an ex-preacher, had visions of reformation for the county that didn't fit in with Rudd's plans. Rudd used his influence in town to coerce the voters.

When they were riding out of town, Rudd explained what he had in mind. It was for McBride to take care of some unfinished business at the far southern end of the county for a few days, at a time that Rudd would name.

"Collecting back taxes," Rudd said. "Things like that. You can find something to keep you busy most of a week."

McBride fingered his flabby chin. "If I'm gone that long, I better appoint a deputy."

"No need," Rudd said hastily. "I'll be in town. Me and my boys will take a hand if there's trouble."

They had reined in, sitting in their saddles in the shade of sycamores. A creek splashed its way through giant rocks, catching the sunlight where it snaked into the open.

"I dunno, Joe," McBride said after a minute. "It seems like you're askin' an awful lot."

But he avoided Rudd's eyes. He'd had trouble holding up his head since the day out at the Rubio Mine when he had fainted dead away. And now as he allowed his eyes to slide across Rudd's face did he read mockery there? The corpulent sheriff swallowed.

"Yeah, I reckon I can do what you want," he said lamely. "You let me know when, Joe."

There was a pained look on the sheriff's face as they rode back to town. Wayfield was in shadow by then and the first lamps were blossoming in windows.

"I'll buy you a dinner, Vince," Rudd said jovially. "Meet you at the hotel in an hour."

"Yeah," McBride grunted and rode away.

Rudd stood looking at McBride's receding figure—a sorry sheriff, for sure, but one that met Rudd's needs.

Eddie Pyne was actually beaming when he came running from the house one morning to catch Lassiter just as he was saddling up.

"What do you think?" Eddie exclaimed.

"Don't know; you tell me," Lassiter said, looking around and wondering at the younger man's ebullience on this crisp morning.

"Eloise is gonna have a baby. *Our* baby!"

"Congratulations," Lassiter managed to say, but he felt less than enthusiastic about a future Pyne heir.

"She's knowed it for about two months but she just got around to tellin' me." A note of complaint killed off some of the exuberance in Eddie's voice. "She was in town yesterday to see the doc. I wondered what the hell for, then she told me."

The next time Lassiter saw Eloise, despite warning himself, his eyes inadvertently swept to her midsection to see if she showed yet. She didn't.

Eloise accepted his congratulations with a shrug and said nothing. Her face showed strain, the skin stretched tight at the temples, her lips squeezed together.

"Eloise, I think between Devlin and me we can scrape up a thousand dollars." It was about all he had left; he knew Devlin had nothing; Devlin could pay him back later. "We'd buy back Eddie's share of DL."

"How about my share, Mr. Lassiter?" she suddenly flashed, peering up into his face, her small hands balled into fists. "Don't I count for *anything?*"

He tried to console her. "Sure you do, but in this country wives don't usually have much of a say about what their husbands do." He knew it was the wrong thing to say the minute he opened his mouth.

"This marriage is different," she said in a tight voice. "I have every right to speak my mind. To share in what my husband has!"

"Tell you one thing," he sighed, "you've got more spunk than I gave you credit for."

"It's about time I got some spunk."

"Maybe the baby coming has helped it along, eh?" he said, thinking it would do no harm to josh her along a bit. But she wasn't humored. She looked him right in the eye.

"I want to hang onto our half of the ranch," she said firmly. "And I think you'll find that Eddie feels the same way."

You'll make sure of that, Lassiter thought.

A morose Lassiter rode to town. There were only a few people on the walks, the hitching racks barely used. Next Saturday was payday and the town then would come alive as cowhands and miners from the surrounding Diablo range rode in for supplies. Or they would hunt for a quick way to get rid of the money they had worked so hard to earn. Lassiter wished mightily he had never seen the place, that he had gone on down into Texas, which had been his destination when he ran into Owney Devlin after so many years. From then on, one thing had led to another and now Lassiter found himself saddled with a ranch and a partner he despised. And how the hell could he cut himself free without saying farewell to the money already invested.

He was turning it all over in his mind while nursing a whiskey in Matt's, the town's other saloon. It was a low-ceilinged place with overhead copper lamps and a floor scarred from spurs and broken bottles. Matt Pell, the owner, a brawny man with a shock of reddish hair, was capable of maintaining order in the rough establishment.

He spoke to Lassiter and they passed the time of day.

Just as Lassiter finished his drink, a heavyset man sidled up to stand beside him at the bar. "You was pointed out to me as partner to Eddie Pyne," the man said bluntly.

Lassiter cautiously admitted this while looking the man over. Although it violated Western ethics to ask a man his name, Lassiter felt that in this case it didn't matter; he didn't like the looks of the stranger.

"Name of Jethro Kaney," the man said in response to Lassiter's taut question. Kaney tipped forward on worn boots, awaiting Lassiter's reaction to mention of the name. There was none. The name while vaguely familiar meant nothing to Lassiter.

Around them were voices from the few drinkers and occasional laughter. "What's on your mind, Kaney?"

"To tell you I'm here for one reason."

"And what's that?"

"To settle up with a gent."

"What gent?"

"Your partner, Eddie Pyne."

"What'd Pyne do to get you riled?" Lassiter drawled.

"I'll let you think about it an' sweat, Lassiter."

Kaney swung around on the sloped heel of his old boot and stepped from Matt's. There he was joined by a younger, shorter man with a scarred face. This one was looking back at the saloon, laughing at something Jethro Kaney had said from a corner of his mouth. Then the two of them marched back along Commerce Street.

Lassiter threw a coin on the bar to pay for his drink.

"You ever see him before, Matt?" Lassiter asked the saloonman.

"Nope," Matt responded. "Got the mark of hard-case on him."

"That's what I was thinking," Lassiter said, took a hitch at his gunbelt and stepped outside. It was a warm day, the sun brassy in a cloudless sky, the air so clear that distant mountains seemed only slightly more than an arm's length away. Birds, startled by the sudden braying of a mule, swirled out of some cedars along the street. They swooped frantically for several seconds, then gathered in a mass and once again disappeared under tree branches.

But Lassiter had eyes only for the pair sauntering

along the walk ahead of him. Their boots thumped on the planks. The younger one glanced back over his shoulder at Lassiter, then leaned to say something to Jethro. But Jethro didn't break stride. Both men disappeared inside the Four Aces.

The swinging doors were still vibrating slightly when Lassiter reached them. The first thing he saw as he entered the place was Joe Rudd at the bar. Standing next to him was diminutive Sid Salone. Kaney and the other man joined Rudd and Salone at the bar. Rudd pushed his bottle toward them and called for two glasses.

Deciding to hang around and see what Rudd was up to with Kaney and the other one, Lassiter found a place at the bar and ordered a whiskey from the dumpy Cavendish with the bushy sideburns.

Rudd, carrying a glass, came up to where Lassiter was standing. "I hear you met Jethro," Rudd said.

"You're the one must've seen me go into Matt's. And told him."

"You're right," Rudd admitted with a tight smile.

"I know I'll likely find out in time, but for the hell of it I'll chip things along a bit by asking. What's it all about, Rudd?" On the last question, Lassiter's voice had hardened.

"Sure I'll tell you." Rudd spoke about Jethro Kaney and his cousin Art coming West all the way from Missouri. "They want to settle up with Eddie Pyne."

"How'd they know where to find Pyne?" Lassiter demanded, watching the bland features of the other man.

Rudd shrugged. "They never said. The main thing is

that Pyne killed Jethro's younger brother. He shot him in the back."

Lassiter didn't even twitch at that news, although he had to admit that back-shooting was probably Eddie Pyne's style. "That's not the way Eddie tells it."

"Course not. Who wants to admit they sneaked behind a barn and blew out a man's backbone?"

"Why're you telling me this?" Lassiter nodded toward Jethro up at the bar, hunched over a glass. "Why not let him tell it?"

"I'm just interested in seeing what Eddie'll do, once you pass the word."

"Do?"

"Yeah, face up to Jethro or tuck tail an' run. And leave behind him a half interest in a good ranch." Rudd bit off the end of a cigar, struck a match, his eyes hard through the flag of yellow flame. "But maybe that's the way you'd like it done."

"How so?"

"Then you'd own all of DL yourself."

"Tell me something. If Jethro Kaney is bent on facing up to Eddie, then why's his cousin Art tagging along?"

"Insurance, you might say. Just to see that everything goes right."

Lassiter was aware that men were staring, as if wondering at the conversation between the two known enemies. Even Art Kaney had turned, thumbs hooked in a vest pocket. A bar of sunlight from a side window rested on the long scar across the side of his face. Lassiter guessed it was made by the slash of a woman's knife, because of its lack of depth.

Rudd leaned forward and began to tap Lassiter on the chest with a long forefinger, obviously to impress upon him a point he was about to make. But Lassiter seized the forefinger, saying, "I don't like what you're doing. I'll break it off at the roots."

Their eyes locked and Rudd's brown ones took on a dangerous glint. But sweat popped out on his forehead as Lassiter bent the finger back. At last he turned him loose.

"The next time don't tap me on the chest," Lassiter said. "I don't like it worth a damn."

Men drinking near them edged quickly away.

Rudd stood, flexing the fingers of his right hand, especially the one Lassiter had treated so roughly.

"Next Saturday is payday," Rudd snarled. "Jethro wants the showdown to be here in town. He wants plenty of witnesses."

"Your idea, you mean."

"To give the folks a little show is Jethro's idea. It'll break the monotony."

"I wonder what McBride will say to your plans," Lassiter said.

"Go ask him."

"I will."

"I s'pose you'll come in with Eddie on Saturday— and likely with Owney Devlin—to see that everything goes right." Rudd wore a faint smile. He was still working the forefinger that Lassiter had bent nearly double.

"We'll see," Lassiter replied.

"If Eddie don't show up in town next Saturday," Rudd said, "then Jethro will know he's nothing but a yellow dog. He'll go looking for him."

But when Lassiter went to ask McBride about the situation, he learned that the sheriff had gone to the southern part of the county to collect back taxes.

A thoughtful Lassiter rode to Apperson's. He took a shortcut past a sloping cliff of smooth rock polished by centuries of storms that had filled it with numerous pockets. The wind in his face tasted of far-off places and he had an urge to flee the Diablo range. But he couldn't just ride off, could he? Leaves of cottonwoods drooped in the midday heat.

By the time he arrived, the sun was westering, its rays shooting through the basket weave of cottonwood branches. He rode out to the shack. Devlin's horse was in a makeshift corral.

"Hullo the house!" he called to the closed front door.

Presently, Devlin flung it open. These days Lassiter always felt a measure of relief when he found his partner sober. Today Devlin was clear-eyed but wearing a two-day stubble of reddish beard.

Ruthie was waiting tables up at Apperson's, Devlin said. And when Lassiter, taking a chair, made no comment, Devlin flushed and said, "It's true. That's *all* she's doin'. We're mostly livin' off the money Allie Kerrington paid me for bustin' horses."

"I believe you, Owney." Then he told him about the Kaneys and their story of how Eddie had killed their kin back in Missouri.

When he had finished, Devlin worked his heavy hands together and stared vacantly across the room at the rusted stove. "Got to admit it sounds more like Eddie," he said heavily, "than him standin' up to a man face to face."

"It may just be Kaney's story," Lassiter put in quickly, not to ease Eddie's burden of guilt but Devlin's pain reflected in his eyes.

"Right or wrong, I figure it's time Eddie took a stand," Devlin said firmly.

"Kaney's got the cold-eyed look of a killer, Owney."

"I'll be on hand to see that nobody climbs Eddie's back." Devlin sounded suddenly tired. Perhaps he was thinking of a life twisted all out of shape just because of his nephew. Nothing had been right since Eddie Pyne had entered their lives.

"You say it's to be Saturday?" Devlin asked heavily. "I got to start keepin' track of the days, Lassiter. I lost count."

"By the way, Eloise is going to have a baby."

It came as a greater shock to Devlin than Lassiter had anticipated. Devlin drew breath and stiffened in his chair as if Lassiter had suddenly drenched him with a bucket of ice water. His eyes squeezed shut. When he opened them, they were wet.

"Had we got married like I planned," he said in a dead voice, "it'd be my kid she's havin', not Eddie's." As if ashamed of tears, Devlin jumped to his feet, brushed his eyes and tromped across the board floor to sweep up the coffee pot kept hot on the back of the stove. He brought back two cups and filled them.

Lassiter took a sip of hot coffee, trying to sort out words tumbling about in his head. "What I'm getting at is this, Owney. Eddie'll be a father before too many months. It'd be a damn shame if the kid's born and never even sees its own father."

"I reckon it would," Devlin agreed with a sigh.

"Here's an idea." It had come to Lassiter suddenly. "You could send Eddie and Eloise away. Maybe over to Prescott."

"With Kaney on his tail?"

Lassiter shook his head. "No. You and me, we'll go to town. We'll explain to Jethro Kaney and his cousin that Eddie isn't around—prod them into making a move. Then if we're lucky, we'll end it then and there."

"What about Sheriff McBride buttin' in?"

Lassiter told him about the sheriff being out of town. "I got a hunch he won't be back till after Saturday. It smells to me of Rudd. But I can't prove it."

"Which means we'd also likely have Rudd an' his foreman to fight. That Salone is a mean-eyed little son of a bitch if I ever seen one."

"What do you say, Owney? Shall I tell Eddie to pack up and get going?"

"What if he won't budge?"

Lassiter gave a soft laugh and without thinking he said, "I think Eddie's yellow clear down to his heels and so do you."

Devlin stiffened in his chair, his broad face losing color. "Eddie'll run if he's given half a chance. You think I oughta talk to him, Lassiter?"

"Wouldn't hurt, I guess," Lassiter replied carefully.

Devlin got a sheet of paper and stub of pencil and sat down to write a note to Ruthie. But he finally gave up. He shoved the paper over to Lassiter who was finishing his coffee. "I don't like to bother her at work an' I don't make my letters so good. An' besides, my hand's shakin' too much. You write it."

Lassiter wrote a note to Ruthie, explaining that Devlin had gone to DL.

"Tell her I'll be back tonight," Devlin put in. "I don't like to leave her alone out here. There's too many hardcases hangin' around."

"I agree," Lassiter said. He got up and within minutes he and Devlin were riding out together.

23

ELOISE PYNE FELT EVERYTHING drain out of her, leaving her completely limp. She clutched the seat brace of the wagon with both hands and turned sideways. She had begged Eddie to take her for a drive, to get away from the house where she felt the tension of Lassiter and the others like a circular wall getting smaller and smaller until finally it would squeeze out her life.

They had been driving along wheeltracks when she saw horsemen coming from the direction of town. The heavyset man who cut away from the others she recognized as Joe Rudd. He cantered up, tipped his hat to her, polite as ever, then turned to Eddie. He began talking about someone named Kaney back in Missouri and how he had been shot in the back.

While Rudd was talking, she looked at Eddie's face and saw that it had drained dead white. The horsemen with Rudd remained out on the flats, mere dots that now seemed to swim before her eyes like liver spots. She felt nausea and attributed it to her pregnancy. But there was more to it than that because Rudd's voice droned on. Eddie had not opened his mouth to refute the damaging charge, but just sat slumped on the wagon seat with his mouth open. The only sounds were Eddie's heavy breathing, the stomp of horses and the crunch of their large teeth on clumps of grass underfoot.

At last Eloise found her voice. "It isn't true, Mr. Rudd. Eddie wouldn't . . . couldn't shoot anyone in the back."

"I'm afraid so, Mrs. Pyne." His gaze danced over her figure, which made her feel as if he had stripped off her clothing. She looked away, her cheeks flaming at the thought.

"I just figured to prepare you, Eddie," Rudd said softly. "They'll be expecting you Saturday. I'll buy you a drink afterwards." This was followed by a hearty slap on Eddie's arm, a tipped hat to Eloise. Then he was riding back to join the others. They headed in the direction of Hayfork. Eddie sagged in the wagon seat as if frozen.

"I suppose it'll mean running," Eloise said, unable to keep contempt from coloring her voice.

Mechanically, Eddie picked up the reins, turned the team and wagon and started back for the ranch house. Only a smudge of color had returned to his cheeks.

"I won't run," Eddie said, taking a deep, shuddering breath. "I won't."

"They'll hunt you down."

"I'll kill 'em."

"Shoot them in the back like you did their kin in Missouri?"

"I never!" he shouted at her.

Eddie's remark caused relief to start flowing through her; he sounded sincere. "Then if you didn't shoot that man in the back, why didn't you speak up?" she wanted to know.

"Rudd . . . he took me by surprise."

"We'll talk to Lassiter and see what he has to say about it," Eloise suggested.

But Eddie turned on her. "Keep your mouth shut to Lassiter!" he said savagely. "I don't want him to know about it!"

"You know he'll find out." She reached for his nearest hand and gave it a squeeze. "I'm sorry I doubted you."

He looked at her out of wild eyes. "Hell of a wife you are!"

"Why do you say that, Eddie?"

"Not believin' your own husband."

"Well, I thought you should have denied it when Mr. Rudd—"

"You're likely sweet on him." Eddie's lips twisted.

"Sweet on him? Never."

"Allie Kerrington is. Everybody says so. Half the women in Wayfield think he's Moses on a cloud."

She edged away from him in the narrow seat as much as possible. "How could you even think that I'm sweet on Mr. Rudd?"

"Cause you believed his lies instead of believin' me."

"But you didn't *say* anything, Eddie. You didn't even open your mouth."

When they got home, Lassiter and Devlin were waiting for them. As she had told Eddie, Lassiter already knew. And so did his uncle.

When Eddie denied the charge made by Jethro Kaney, Devlin lost his temper. "Admit it, you snivelin' little . . ."

A backhand crashed into Eddie's face, still not quite healed from the last raging attack by his uncle.

Eloise tried desperately to grab Devlin's thick arm, but he shoved her away. There were other backhands that finally drove him to his knees. His blood dripped into the dust. The ranch hands had come to form a silent circle.

"I . . . I . . . done it," Eddie babbled at last. "I was scared that if I didn't, he'd kill me."

Despair ripped through Eloise like a knife. Woodenly, she turned and walked stiffly across the yard and entered the house. The door closed quietly behind her.

Later Eddie came in and lay beside her on the bed where she had flung herself. Desperately, he tried to explain the power of the Kaneys back in Missouri, how he would be dead now if Jethro and his cousin hadn't been locked up in jail at the time. Had they been free, Eddie continued, he would never have married Eloise, never fathered her child.

"Don't you see? I shot him to protect myself!" he pleaded.

"You could have left town," she pointed out in a dead voice.

"I . . . couldn't. There was my aunt's house an' her things, an' with her just dead it meant money for me."

As he talked, his hand slid along her leg but she caught his wrist and said, "No, Eddie. I forgot to tell you, but the doctor said no. Not until after the baby is born."

It was her own lie but she felt justified in closing herself off from her husband—the liar, the coward, the murderer.

It crossed her mind to take a gun and put the barrel in her mouth and pull the trigger, taking her own life and that of her unborn child. Better that than to have the child come into the world with Eddie as a father.

But that was cowardly and she couldn't bring herself to such an ugly and irrevocable step. No, she would go on. There must be some good in Eddie *somewhere,* she told herself.

She sat up on the bed. Eddie had left the room, slamming the door behind him. From where she was sitting she could see Lassiter and Devlin in the yard, talking together. For the first time, she studied Devlin objectively, not in fear as she had when first meeting him in Wayfield shortly after Lassiter had deposited the body of a dead man on the walk in front of the sheriff's office. She thought about those few awkward times afterward when he visited her in town. After that, Eddie courting her, quickly tearing down her fences. Weak female that I was, she thought bitterly.

Owney, my dear, she thought as she watched him in the yard, if only you hadn't sent Eddie to town to comfort me I could have grown to care for you.

Her eyes stung and she wiped them on a corner of the blanket. She looked around at fresh paint on the walls, the windows she heard had been replaced, sections of the floor that had been repaired. Owney Devlin had done it all for her, with the exuberance of a schoolboy, Lassiter had told her once.

And she had thrown it all away in one blinding burst of passion.

24

NEWS OF THE SHOWDOWN Saturday finally trickled out to K-27 where Allie Kerrington digested it soberly. "It looks as if Eddie Pyne tried his sneaky tricks once too often," she told her foreman, Davey Prince.

Prince ran his fingers through his graying hair and looked toward the horizon where the setting sun rested elliptically before its plunge into the abyss of night.

"Eddie Pyne ain't got a chance, Miss Kerrington. My guess is that by Saturday he'll be miles away from Wayfield."

"I shouldn't wonder," she said.

"I wish that damn Lassiter . . ." Her head swung around and she gave him a sharp glance. "Oh, never mind," he finished with a weary gesture.

"Go ahead, finish it, Davey."

"I wish he'd come over here . . . where he belongs."

"So do I," she sighed. "I wish it very much." And she transferred the wish to the first star still dim in the fading light. Oh, Lassiter, why are you so bullheaded?

"Eat with me tonight, Davey. I'm tired of being alone."

"I'd like that," he said, with a faint hope in his eyes. But secretly he knew she'd never marry him. He had worshiped her as a growing child, seen her shipped off to school in the East. He'd been here when her betrothed tried to learn the cattle business and found a grave instead.

"And during dinner tell me about the old days here, Davey," she said with a small smile. "Remind me of how great we were once." Bitterness tinged her voice.

"Are you goin' to town Saturday?"

"I don't want to go." Her shoulders drooped. "But we'll see." An hour later when she was fixing supper, she heard the sounds of a horse in the yard. Running to the window, her heart pounding, she wondered if it could be possible. It was. Lassiter bounded up the veranda steps.

She flung open the door and rushed into his arms. "Lassiter, Lassiter. I've been thinking so much about you lately."

He held her at arm's length, looking down into her pretty face. "I just got a sudden itch to see you, Allie."

"I love that itch." They both laughed.

Davey came along the path just then from the bunk-house and saw them standing together on the porch.

"Oh, I heard a horse, but didn't know you had company," he said. "Evenin', Lassiter."

"Howdy."

"Come in and join us, Davey," Allie urged. "You're still welcome."

"I reckon I'll eat in the bunkhouse." Turning on his heel, he hurried back into the shadowed cottonwoods and disappeared.

"What was that all about?" Lassiter asked as they entered the house arm in arm.

"I was lonely. I asked Davey to eat supper with me. I hope his feelings aren't hurt. But am I glad we'll be alone."

He set the table for her while she ladled a fine stew into brown bowls.

Later, as they lay together in the rumpled bed, the scene of their frenzied reunion, she asked what had really prompted him to call on her.

"I got to thinking that life is so damn short." He sighed deeply. "I wanted to see you again is all."

"You're thinking about Saturday . . . in town, aren't you?"

He was silent for a few moments, staring up at the moon-swept ceiling. In the distance, coyotes howled at the night in competition with the softer hoot of an owl.

"So you know about Saturday," he said, trying to keep his voice straight.

She sat up in bed, staring down at him on his back, fingers locked behind his dark head. "You know what I think?" she said.

"No. Just what do you think?"

"You're going to side with Eddie Pyne." She could barely get it out.

"I got a hunch that's what Devlin figures to do," he told her.

"Then let him. After all, Eddie's his nephew."

"But Devlin's my partner."

"That doesn't mean you have to risk your neck for him."

"I aim to be there and keep anybody from jumping on his back."

"But it isn't your fight, Lassiter."

"I'll say it again. Devlin's my partner. I owe him my loyalty."

"Eddie did a cowardly thing by shooting a man in the back. If what I hear is true, and I assume it is."

"Makes no difference, Allie."

"It's what you meant by life being so damn short. Isn't it, Lassiter?"

"Maybe."

Her lower lip began to tremble. "Oh, Lassiter . . ."

He tried to explain about Eloise carrying Eddie's child. "Eddie's going to be a father. Both Devlin and I figure it's what he needs to settle him down."

"I'm not so sure it won't take more than that."

"I've looked the Kaneys over. They're not much. Eddie says they were serving a year in jail for beating a man half to death over a horse trade."

"You can't believe anything Eddie Pyne says."

"They've got the mark of killer on them. I know the breed. And Rudd has sweet-talked the sheriff into being out of town Saturday, which makes it worse."

"I've got a hollow feeling in my stomach, Lassiter. I'm scared."

He pulled her down on top of him. "I can fix that," he teased against her ear. Then he gently bit her earlobe, which caused her to twitch. Her eyes glowed strangely in the moonlight.

"I guess it's a good thing you won't marry me," she said lightly. "You'd soon wear me down to skin and bones."

His lips, seeking her mouth, closed off further speech.

On Friday, Lassiter had a visitor at DL. It was Parkie Dolan, a gaunt man who never had much to say. He had ridden over from his ranch alone. At first Lassiter was wary because Dolan was a member of the Hayfork pool.

Dolan came right to the point. "Some of us is gettin' worried about Rudd. I ain't sayin' which ones."

"Worried? In what way?"

"Rudd's already feelin' his biscuits. If he gets any more power, it'll be bad for all of us."

"What're you getting at?"

"If there's any way you can be helped out Saturday, speak up."

"Stay home," Lassiter said. "That'll be a help."

"Rudd's already sent word he wants us in town. With our guns." Dolan looked Lassiter in the eye.

Lassiter thought about it. "What if we played a trick on Mr. Joe Rudd?"

"How you figure to do that?"

Lassiter clapped him on the arm and smiled. "Come into the bunkhouse for some coffee and we'll talk about it."

25

THE BEST-LAID PLANS OF mice and men and gunfighters and their ladies are apt to go awry. . . .

Saturday was a September blazer with the coppery sun taking one last stab at summer. Those who arrived early in town sought pools of shadow. Horses steamed and bandannas for mopping moist brows were much in evidence. A thread of excitement ran through Wayfield on that early morning, intensified when men gathered along the street spread the word to new arrivals or ducked into the store or saloon to give the latest news.

"Eddie Pyne's ridin' in with his uncle an' Lassiter."

From out of heat haze and dust materialized the DL wagon, Eddie Pyne handling the reins. At his side was his wife, equally pale as her husband, a small bonnet pinned to her hair. They sat stiffly on the wagon seat, their bodies jolting from the ruts and bumps of the road, the team prancing along smartly.

Flanking the wagon were Devlin and Lassiter, the latter's head turning at every few steps of his black horse as if to seek out a potential ambush. Never had he looked more formidable with the butt of a .44 jiggling at his thigh.

Allie Kerrington, on the walk in front of the hotel, let out a long-held breath, staring as if it might be the last time she'd see him. She was equally as pale as Eloise and Eddie Pyne. The wagon pulled past the hotel and into the turnaround of the Wayfield Store. The team was tied. Lassiter and Devlin racked their horses alongside. It was very quiet. All eyes were on them. A man coughing across the street seemed unusually loud.

Without a word, Eloise climbed from the wagon before anyone could give her a hand. She marched up the steps of the loading platform and into the store. There she tarried a minute, one eye on her husband and his uncle and Lassiter in the yard. Then she left by the front door and hurried across the street before anyone could stop her.

A buzz of voices in the Four Aces drained to absolute stillness as she entered and stood looking around at the slightly startled faces; a lady did not enter a saloon the caliber of the Four Aces.

"Is Mr. Jethro Kaney here?" she asked in a firm voice.

Every eye was fastened on the pretty Mrs. Pyne with the pale hair and light blue eyes. Her chin was lifted above a pale yellow dress with white cuffs, her small hands at her sides clenched into fists.

"Here, ma'am," said Kaney, stepping out from the crowded bar to stand with hands on hips, a twisted smile on his lips.

"May I speak to you alone, Mr. Kaney?"

"You got anything to say, ma'am, say it here."

"But I . . . I'd rather . . ." Her hands started to tremble but she drew them into tighter fists.

Kaney half turned back to the bar, his smile broad, his wink dancing along the faces of onlookers.

"Wait," she said. "All right, I'll speak. I'm here to ask you—no, to beg you—to leave my husband alone."

"I came a far piece to settle with him."

"I . . . I'm going to have a baby. Don't deprive my child of his father."

Heads swiveled from her to Kaney who now said roughly, "You're askin' too much, ma'am."

Brassy sunlight cutting through side windows settled on her eyes, which were beginning to brim with tears. *"Please . . ."*

Kaney's smile vanished. "He shot my brother in the back. At least I'm willin' to meet him face up. That's more'n he did with Clyde."

Joe Rudd, who was standing with Art Kaney and Sid Salone, detached himself from the bar and walked over to her, his boots thumping the plank floor. He removed his hat and gave a little bow, looking elegant in tan riding clothes. The gold chain across his middle sparkled in the sunlight.

"Madam, did your husband send you to beg for his life?" Rudd asked politely.

"He knows nothing about it."

"Then . . ."

Rudd was interrupted. At that moment, a wild-eyed Eddie Pyne, a holstered .45 at his belt, pushed through the doors. He slid to a halt when he saw the tableau:

his wife, rigid and pale, facing Rudd and a man he knew to be Kaney. He had Clyde's eyes and sneering mouth.

"Eloise, damn it, I let you come along 'cause you promised you wouldn't butt in. . . ." His voice died away to a whisper as Kaney's eyes burned into his face from halfway across the big room. There wasn't a sound in the saloon lined with men frozen in various postures of fear and anticipation. A situation as deadly as a lake of spilled kerosene and some careless person with a single flaring match.

"You got ten minutes, Pyne," Kaney's voice cut through the stillness. "Then I'll see you outside. In the street."

Lassiter and Devlin came crashing in at that moment.

"What's goin' on?" Devlin cried, his large head swinging from Eddie and Eloise to Rudd and Kaney.

Lassiter got Eloise by an arm and felt her tremble. He backed with her to the doors, never taking his eyes from Kaney or Rudd, or Art Kaney and Sid Salone at the bar. He backed up with Eloise through the doors.

And when the doors flapped back into place, he said, "That was a damn fool thing you did, Mrs. Pyne."

"I tried. I only tried." Her teeth chattered despite the warm day.

"I was against you coming along in the first place."

Eddie Pyne walked outside stiff-legged as if drunk, although there was no odor of whiskey on his breath. He had to clear his throat several times to get his voice straightened out before speaking.

"I'm gonna face up to him, I told you that," he said in a brassy voice filled with insincere bravado.

Every eye on the street was on them and even the saloon windows were now jammed with faces.

"You can't go through with facin' up to him, Eddie," Devlin said tensely when they had walked away from the saloon entrance to stand on a street corner.

"I can, I *can!*" It was almost a sob, Lassiter noticed. Devlin and his nephew argued and shouted. Devlin finally gave up.

"All right, Eddie, if that's the way you want it," he said after a few moments.

Eloise turned her rigid body so that she faced Devlin on the street. "I know you no longer have any feeling for me, Owney," Eloise said shakily, "but for the sake of Eddie's unborn child, if for no other reason, don't let him do this."

Devlin looked at her long and grimly and with a trace of hurt. He blinked and turned to his nephew who was staring fixedly at mountains where sunlight splashed on granite cliffs.

"I . . . I can't stop him if it's what he's bound to do," Devlin said and placed a hand on Eddie's arm. "An' if he makes it . . . no, I'll change that. *When* he makes it, I'll be so goddamn proud of him . . ." Devlin's voice cracked. "Let me tell you one thing, Eddie. Just before you figure Kaney's gonna make his move, throw yourself flat."

Eddie looked at his uncle. "Flat?"

"Flat in the street. It'll throw him off guard, for one thing. Take him by surprise." Devlin's voice was shrill now with excitement. "An' that way you won't give him as much target to shoot at as you would if you was still on your feet."

"I . . . I see." Eddie wiped his mouth on the back of his hand. Today he wore a faded work shirt and Levis.

"And as you're goin' down, Eddie, you draw your gun. Understand?"

"Yeah . . . yeah . . ." Eddie's eyes grew round.

"But get two hands on the gun, not one. It'll steady the barrel. All you'll need is one shot." Devlin's teeth were bared fiercely.

"Two hands?"

"Grip the gun with your right, steady it with the left. I've seen it done once. In Chihuahua City. A *pistolero.* You remember, Lassiter."

"Sorry, I wasn't there."

"But it'll work," Devlin said fervently. "I know it will."

Lassiter was careful not to commit himself. Devlin was giving his nephew an awful lot to digest all in a few minutes.

"Owney!" It was Ruthie, wearing her blue dress, the hem hiked halfway up her legs as she rode a sorrel up the crowded street.

"I told you to stay out of it," Devlin wailed.

She swung down, ran lightly to him, grinning up into his face. Although she no longer plied her trade at Apperson's, waiting on tables and singing only, on this day her face was generously splashed with color—lips rouged, cheeks reddened, eyebrows darkened.

Devlin got Eloise and Ruthie each by an arm. "You ladies go on into the hotel where you'll be safe, hear?" He gave them a gentle shove in that direction.

Eloise, moving away, cast Devlin a strange look

over her shoulder. Was it regret? Lassiter couldn't quite decide.

The tension was so great along the street that a sudden snarling dog fight made everyone jump. Some men got the dogs separated. The sudden quiet was awesome.

"Ten minutes is about up," a man said nervously over the tops of the saloon doors to those waiting tensely on the outside.

Men began to gingerly move away from the swinging doors.

Eloise turned stiffly and waved to Eddie, but he wasn't looking in her direction. She went on to the hotel, her steps dragging. Ruthie, refusing to budge, remained at Devlin's side.

At that moment, Joe Rudd stepped scowling from the Four Aces to peer along the street.

Lassiter said, "Lost something?"

Rudd turned on him and saw the sardonic smile. "I expected members of the Hayfork pool to be in town for the big event," he said through his teeth. "But I see they're not."

"So." Lassiter lifted a shoulder.

"You know anything about it, Lassiter?"

"Only that they're down at Matt's. They were given word that that's where you wanted to meet them."

Rudd snarled an oath and glanced at Matt's Saloon at the far east end of Commerce Street, noting the horses bunched at the rack there.

He started in that direction but had taken no more than two steps when Lassiter said, "I wouldn't if I was you. My men have 'em corraled. And Tom Hefter's shotgun is a mighty good persuader."

Rudd halted and swung around. "Goddamn you, Lassiter." His face reddened, the eyes narrowed and he drew himself up on his toes. "Why'd you butt in today, anyhow?"

"To trim the odds a little is why."

"This won't be your lucky day, Lassiter."

"Nor yours. I'm remembering rustled cattle on the day of Ruthie's trial, to keep me busy and out of town."

Rudd elbowed his way toward the Four Aces.

Down at the far end of Commerce Street, Tom Hefter risked a glance out Matt's window and saw the distant knot of people in front of the Four Aces. It was too far to make out faces, but he guessed who was present. Although he had no use for Eddie Pyne, he said a little prayer for his safety this day, more for Eloise and the baby she carried than for Eddie.

The brawny Matt Pell stood behind his bar with thick arms folded across his chest. He seemed mildly amused at the twelve men lined up against the far wall—four scowling members of the Hayfork pool and a scattering of their hands. Their weapons, a saddle rope run through the trigger guards, were in a heap at Hefter's feet. The other four DL men stood next to Hefter, their guns drawn.

Doc Plane, not so courtly today, snarled an oath. "You hadn't oughta side in with 'em, Matt," he said angrily.

Matt laughed at the pool member. "You boys used to do your drinkin' in here. But Rudd snaps his fingers an' now it's the Four Aces."

"Still, you could kick these DL hombres outa your place of business."

"An' face up to that shotgun?" Matt shook his large head crowned with reddish hair. "No siree, not me."

He winked at Tom Hefter with the shotgun. Hefter smiled. Sharing in the smile was Parkie Dolan who stood with his back to the wall alongside the other members of the Hayfork pool.

The smile on Hefter's lips faded as he noticed from a corner of his eye a commotion up by the Four Aces.

26

In view of what happened later, one man said that when Jethro Kaney finally stepped from the Four Aces it was the same as hell's front door blown open with a burst of powder and flame.

Kaney was followed outside by his cousin Art and Sid Salone, the Hayfork foreman. That morning Jethro had visited the barber. His cheeks were lightly dusted with talc.

He was in his shirt sleeves, his big gun strapped low on his right leg. His lips were twisted in a faint smile. When his eyes locked on Eddie Pyne's face, Lassiter tensed. He wondered at Eddie's reaction, halfway expecting the younger man to beg for his life. But Eddie didn't open his mouth. He stood stiffly with shoulders back, not meeting Kaney's hard eyes, but still not flinching.

In spite of everything, Lassiter felt a grudging respect for Devlin's nephew.

Jethro Kaney's smile for Eddie Pyne was superior.

"I'll go up to the corner an' start back along the street," he said in his heavy, faintly mocking voice. "Make your play any time you're ready."

"Yeah, I . . . I understand.".

"Only wait till I'm facin' you," Jethro went on. "Not in the back like you done my kid brother Clyde."

At this, a murmur of voices rippled along the street. Kaney brushed disdainfully past a rigid Eddie Pyne and sauntered on up to the corner. Nearby on a side street was the sheriff's office, tightly closed, a penciled scrawl in the window: GONE ON BUSINESS.

Devlin got his nephew by an arm. "Remember what I told you."

"I . . . I'll remember."

"He's had whiskey an' you've had none. Whiskey slows a man. I oughta know."

Eddie Pyne gave his uncle a nod. Then he walked out into the center of the street, his face ashen.

"You can do it, Eddie," Devlin called.

Kaney made his turn and started back along the street, still wearing that smile, strolling as if to a picnic, not a possible rendezvous with death. At that point the crowd thinned, men ducking into slots between buildings, alleys, to get away from potential danger, but still wanting to witness it. Those backed against building fronts were rigid, every breath held tight in aching lungs.

The way Eddie Pyne was standing in the center of the street, his right hand loose at his side, his hand near his gun, caused Jethro Kaney to miss a step. He no longer wore his smile, but now looked faintly concerned. He pulled his hat brim low to cut the sun, probably wishing now he'd chosen the other direction without the sun in his eyes. Pyne seemed determined to make a fight of it after all.

"Any time, Pyne," Kaney sang out.

As the tension along Commerce Street grew almost unbearable now that Kaney had halted, the slender figure of Eddie Pyne suddenly jackknifed. He vomited in the center of the street. Then he spun around and, wiping his mouth on the back of a hand, ran screaming away from Kaney.

"I . . . I can't do it!" he cried.

Kaney drew and fired twice. Eddie's head suddenly drooped, a spot of blood appearing at the back of his neck. The second shot was drilled straight into his back, making a slight pucker in his faded-blue work shirt. He took a few stumbling steps, then crashed into the street.

With a little cry, Ruthie sprang from the crowd in front of the Four Aces and, skirts and hair flying, ran directly to where Eddie was crumpled.

"I'll tend to him, Owney!" she screamed over her shoulder to a stunned Owney Devlin.

It was to be the last sound she ever uttered. No one was ever sure whether Kaney fired deliberately or was still so intent on putting one more bullet into Eddie Pyne that Ruthie became a victim when she got in the way. Jethro's shot jerked her head and brought a gush of blood spilling down the side of her face. She collapsed across Eddie Pyne. A breeze stirred her skirts.

In that handful of seconds, Lassiter saw the shocked faces of onlookers. Devlin uttered a strangled cry of grief and rushed Jethro Kaney in the center of the street.

But it was Art Kaney who fired. Devlin took a staggering step and went down at the edge of the street.

Lassiter spun and was close enough to grab Art Kaney's gun, which was swinging his way. As its hammer came down, he knocked the weapon aside and fired a bullet into the man's chest. It sent Art crashing back into the double doors of the saloon, his mouth sagging.

"Get Lassiter!" Rudd was yelling. Men began to run for cover as bullets whistled dangerously close. Lassiter was ducking low, zigzagging as he ran into the street.

A man screamed, "Kill 'em, Lassiter, for what they done to the gal! Kill 'em all!"

And the cry was taken up. Not too many days ago, some of these same men had been eager to hang Ruthie for a murder she hadn't committed. And now they were yelling for the blood of her killer, forgetting in their excitement that only Jethro Kaney had been responsible. But Rudd and his foreman, Salone, were caught up in a plan to eliminate Lassiter, which brought them to the attention of the crowd. Devlin, the other half of the Lassiter team, was already down.

Jethro Kaney shouted something to Rudd in a high-pitched voice that Lassiter couldn't make out above all the commotion. Lassiter tripped on a street rut as Kaney fired at him, missed, the bullet clanging off a metal sign above the entrance to the Four Aces. There men were sprawling over each other and the body of Art Kaney in their frenzy to get out of the way of stray bullets.

After firing, Kaney ducked sideways, a shifting target. But in so doing, Lassiter's snapped-off shot, intended for the chest, took him in the throat instead. Kaney was bent that low. A great arc of blood from a shattered jugular vein put a startled look in Kaney's eyes before he sagged into the street.

As if on signal, Rudd and Salone fled into the hotel and began firing from the doorway. But Lassiter, in the center of the street, gambled. He sprang for the hotel veranda, which was a good four feet above the street and ducked low. Spurts of dust and hard soil were kicked up in the half of the street he had just crossed. Luckily, none of the bullets hit home. But he felt the breath of some pass his ear.

After a moment, when firing ceased, Lassiter risked a glance. Rudd and his foreman had vanished from the hotel doorway. Lassiter could now hear their pounding boots deeper in the hotel. Hooking his fingers over the veranda railing, he pulled himself up and over, his boots thudding against the porch. Without the crash of guns, a strange quiet had settled over the town.

As he dashed into the hotel, almost too late Lassiter spotted from a corner of his eye, the slight figure of Sid Salone in the kitchen doorway. He saw the glittering eyes in the small face as he swung aside. And as he moved, something crashed into him, driving him to one knee. But in the moment of impact, he fired instinctively. Salone's small frame no longer even partially filled the kitchen doorway. Lassiter glimpsed a terrified cook peering around a heavy pot from which steam was rising.

Lassiter lowered his gaze and saw Salone flat on his

back. A dark wetness was beginning to spread just above the belt buckle. Lassiter, breathing hard, leaned against the doorway. Salone had dropped his gun. Lassiter found he had strength enough left to kick it under the big stove.

Then Lassiter noticed that Salone's eyes were open, his lips trembling. He was trying to speak. At last he got it out. "I'm . . . I'm sorry . . . about the gal. . . ." Then his eyes rolled, the body arched and there came a familiar rattling sound from the throat. Having heard it so many times in his turbulent career in the West, Lassiter didn't need to be told it was a death rattle.

"Rudd's in the store!" A man yelled hysterically from the lobby and waved a long arm in the direction of the Wayfield Store.

Knowing he would have to end it, before there could be any peace on Diablo range, Lassiter staggered out the side door.

"Be careful, Lassiter!" someone shouted through cupped hands from the street.

"Advice," Lassiter muttered, "but no one with guts enough to take a hand."

As he started walking, the two-story building that housed the store seemed to tilt and a grayness started edging in. Desperately, he fought it off. Up the steps of the loading platform he stumbled. He could see a knot of people across the street, some women, all white-faced, staring.

"He's been hit!" he dimly heard someone yell.

He wondered vaguely who had been hit. Then he realized they must have meant him. As he crept along the loading platform, he was suddenly aware of a wetness along his left side. It leaked down his leg and into his boot. He had no idea how long the condition had existed.

He halted and took a deep breath that hurt. In the distance, the great rock walls of mountains in the dazzling sunlight seemed to waver. He turned and, through a corner of a store side window, saw Rudd crouched behind a counter. One of his hands gripped Mary Taleson by an arm. The woman's seamed face, framed in frizzled graying hair, seemed about to collapse. The eyes were large and frightened.

Rudd was facing the side door that Lassiter would have entered had he not paused for that long breath. And had he done so, he now would be awash in his own blood, not that he wasn't to an extent already.

Reaching out with his gun, Lassiter broke a pane of glass with the muzzle, the sound bringing Rudd's head swinging around. The woman saw him and uttered an unearthly scream and tried to pull free of Rudd's hold on her arm.

Lassiter fired, careful not to hit the woman. But it was too quick and he missed. Because Rudd was moving. He dragged the woman from behind the counter, but she showed her mettle by clawing with her nails like a cat. The right side of Rudd's face was suddenly streaked with blood.

A howl of pain burst from his lips. Somehow the woman got away and started running toward the rear of the store.

"Keep down, ma'am!" Lassiter thought he was shouting, but the voice to his own ears seemed strangely weak.

The woman knelt beside her husband who lay face

down on the floor. There was a bloodied gash at the back of his skull where Rudd had evidently struck him with a gun barrel.

By then, Rudd was pounding up a twisting, narrow flight of stairs that led to the second floor.

"You're in no shape to go after him, Lassiter!" Mary Taleson cried as she worked to revive her husband.

But Lassiter made no reply. He was taking time to eject shells from his gun, the empties popping around on the floor. How many dead did they represent? he wondered numbly. Art Kaney and Jethro and Salone. . . .

With hands strangely cold and shaking, he thumbed in fresh bullets. He began to climb the stairs, thinking that Eloise deserved a chance with her baby and if Rudd lived, he'd lean on her.

At the second floor he paused, looking around. He saw two rooms, both with open doors. One was fitted up as an office with rolltop desk and leather chairs. The other was a bedroom, with rumpled bedclothes. Which one was Rudd in?

From a narrow second-floor window in the hall he could look down into the street. The bodies of Ruthie and Eddie had been separated but still lay pretty much as they had fallen. Devlin had been pulled from the street. Did that mean he still lived? Jethro Kaney lay on his back, drained from the severed jugular. He couldn't see Art Kaney's body, probably because of the crowd around the saloon doors. There and along the street, the eyes of onlookers were fixed on the Wayfield Store. Many stood with mouths open.

"Rudd," Lassiter called softly when hearing no

sound from either room. From downstairs came the sounds of Josh Taleson just coming around and his wife's joyful relief.

Lassiter's attention was drawn to a shaft of sunlight. He moved in that direction. He looked up. A ladder led to the roof. A trapdoor was open. He could hear someone tiptoeing around on the roof.

For the first time, as he climbed, he felt sharp pain instead of numbness. Pausing at the top of the ladder, he saw Rudd. The man was poised, as if about to leap across a narrow slot to the roof of the adjoining building.

At that moment, Rudd turned his head and saw Lassiter just emerging to the roof. He fired, at the same time fighting for balance at the roof edge. The impact of the bullet drilling roof planks jolted Lassiter's heels. Rudd's body arched. He dropped his gun.

Lassiter lunged, despite the pain he felt. He reached out with a long right arm. His fingers clamped around Rudd's ankle. It was Lassiter's intention to haul him back to the roof and settle it face to face.

But Rudd screamed, his arms windmilling. He started to fall, Lassiter still gripping him by his ankle. Despite the tremendous weight, Lassiter clung to him. When Rudd's body, at the end of Lassiter's arm, slammed against the building wall, the hold was broken. He yelled all the way down, clawing air wildly. A sodden thump below ended it.

As men suddenly found their voices and streamed across the street, Lassiter looked down over the roof edge. Rudd lay on his right side, the head bent queerly back. Then Lassiter found himself lying on the roof, staring straight up. He closed his eyes against the sun's glare. But suddenly there was no need. Everything was darkness.

Lassiter regained consciousness in the office of Ambrose Hamilton, M.D., where he had been carried. He could see a bank of faces peering in at the window. Allie Kerrington, looking concerned, stood beside his bed.

"You were so incredibly . . . incredibly lucky, Lassiter." She began to cry.

A grave Doc Hamilton was bandaging Lassiter's side.

"How bad is it, Doc?" Lassiter asked, amazed at how difficult it was to form words. Even the effort of speech was trying.

"A bullet ripped up your side and nicked a couple of ribs. An inch over and it would have been deflected into a lung, probably. You lost a lot of blood. As Miss Kerrington says, you're incredibly lucky."

"And the others?"

"Art and Jethro Kaney, dead. Salone dead. Rudd fell off the store roof. Broken neck."

"Devlin?"

"He'll live. He's in the next room."

That was heartening news to Lassiter but he was too weary to do anything about it.

Shortly before noon the following day, Eloise visited Lassiter. From a straight-backed chair beside the bed, she told how she had just buried her husband. She was red-eyed, her pretty face showing strain.

"Eddie was trying to straighten himself up," she said after a few moments of idle talk.

"Yeah, I'm sure he was." Lassiter didn't know what else to say.

"For instance, he was going to confess that the money we were going to use when we ran away, he had stolen from his uncle. He intended to pay it back. He was on the way to paying for most of his past mistakes." She shuddered. "In a way, I'm to blame for his death."

"That's foolish talk, Eloise," Lassiter said gently.

"I shouldn't have insisted we stay here and try to make a go of DL. If we'd gone away, Kaney might never have found him."

"Chances are he'd have tracked him down sooner or later."

"I guess for the baby's sake more than anything else, Eddie was trying." She closed her eyes. "Now what happens? A widow with an unborn child." She gave a weary gesture.

After Eloise left, Tom Hefter and the men trooped in to see how he was getting along. He asked them to look out for Eloise and they promised they would.

Before being driven out to K-27 to recuperate, Lassiter had a long talk with Owney Devlin. The subject, marrying Eloise and being a father to her unborn child. At first, Devlin was stiff-necked about it, but Lassiter persisted.

"I know you're bitter about her and Eddie going behind your back. But you've got to remember she's young and she was scared. . . ."

"No excuse."

"She was set down in the West. And right off she saw that man I killed, Tex Stillway. That broke her to pieces. And you busy working on the house instead of tending to her. Face up to it, Owney; you're the one who threw them together."

After a long silence between them, Lassiter said, "Eddie was your sister Rose's boy. So there'll be part of her in that baby. Forget what's happened and the two of you go on and make new lives for yourselves."

Devlin, his right arm in a sling, sat beside Lassiter's bed, his feet on a chair. He was thinking over what Lassiter had said. "What if Eloise won't have me?"

"You got her once. You convinced her to come out here all the way from St. Louis."

"That was different . . ."

"When you sell cows in the spring you can pay me off. Then you'll own DL, you and Eloise. That's partner enough for you to have."

"And what about you, Lassiter?"

"I'll help out Allie Kerrington. At least until spring. Then we'll see."

Allie Kerrington, wearing a green dress to match her eyes, knocked lightly on the half-open door. Devlin gave her a smile and left the room.

"Lassiter, I've come to take you home," she announced.

"Home being exactly where?"

"My place, as if you didn't know. And, for your information, it'll be a lot later than spring before I'll let you go."

"So you had your ear to the door."

She leaned down and kissed him on the mouth.

Later in the month there was an inquest. It was the judgment of the jury that the deaths attributed to the man known as Lassiter had been justified.

Spectators cheered when the verdict was announced.

Lassiter still wore a bulky bandage and still walked slightly hunched. He waved to everyone as Allie slipped an arm through his and walked with him from the Wayfield Store where the inquest had been held. Clouds dimmed the sun, putting the town in shadow.

Ed Cavendish of the Four Aces caught up with them. "Lassiter, you could run for sheriff an' be elected. Folks are sick of McBride."

"Don't give him any ideas," Allie said quickly. "He'll have job enough running K-27."

Lassiter patted her hand. "I wouldn't be surprised." But his eyes were on the far horizon, shrouded in a tremendous bank of clouds. And he seemed to be saying, I wonder what's beyond. . . .

MAX BRAND®

THE BRIGHT FACE OF DANGER

Through the years, James Geraldi has proven to be one of Max Brand's most exciting and enduring characters, and this volume contains three of his greatest exploits. Geraldi has been dubbed the "Frigate Bird" because of his habit of stealing from thieves, and Edgar Asprey knows just how apt the name is. Geraldi once prevented Asprey from swindling his family out of a fortune, and managed to get rich doing it. That's exactly why Asprey now wants to form an alliance with him. Asprey has his eye on a rare, invaluable treasure, and he knows no one stands a better chance of stealing it than his old enemy, the Frigate Bird.

THE ADVENTURES OF COMANCHE JOHN

DAN CUSHMAN

Comanche John is a notorious road agent. If he has a last name, no one knows it. Yet his legend precedes him in the form of frontier ballads sung by teamsters and stagecoach drivers. His life is filled with danger and conflict, and although his activities often place him on the wrong side of the law, more often than not he ends up defending the innocent and fighting for what's right. *The Adventures of Comanche John* brings the reader into the thrilling world of Montana mining camps, wagon trains on the Oregon Trail, and stagecoaches everywhere.

Dorchester Publishing Co., Inc.
P.O. Box 6640 ___5265-2
Wayne, PA 19087-8640 $4.99 US/$6.99 CAN

Please add $2.50 for shipping and handling for the first book and $.75 for each additional book. NY and PA residents, add appropriate sales tax. No cash, stamps, or CODs. Canadian orders require $2.00 for shipping and handling and must be paid in U.S. dollars. Prices and availability subject to change. **Payment must accompany all orders.**

Name: _____

Address: _____

City: _____ State:_____ Zip: _____

E-mail: _____

I have enclosed $_____ in payment for the checked book(s).

For more information on these books, check out our website at www.dorchesterpub.com.
_____ *Please send me a free catalog.*

— THE —
MEXICAN SADDLE
BENNETT FOSTER

Trail partners Jim and Waco have only a hundred dollars between them. Then Jim lends *that* to another ranch hand, who leaves him an old Mexican saddle as security. The next day, the ranch hand's body is found, mutilated, his hands tied behind his back. Suddenly, Waco runs into a ranchman who wants very much to buy Jim's saddle. Waco sells it to him, only to find soon enough that it isn't Jim's saddle the ranchman wanted after all, but the Mexican saddle Jim had been given as security. Now it seems like a whole lot of people want that saddle. But why? And why are they willing to kill for it?